HELL'S HIGHWAY

THE DEVIL'S DAUGHTER (BOOK 3)

G.A. CHASE

BAYOU MOON PRESS, LLC

ABOUT THIS BOOK

Having put down the latest batch of escaped doppelgängers, Sere Mal-Laurette felt she'd earned a little time off from demon hunting. She was wrong.

Her inattention has allowed a new batch of hellions to rise from the swamp and abduct Rampart Thibodaux. With the hot ex-Navy SEAL's blood and soul infecting her, Sere has no choice but to jump back on her motorcycle to rescue him. Her quest will cost her dearly but also bring her closer to being human than she could have imagined.

Sere's emotional roller-coaster ride of human experiences, however, is overshadowed by the rise of a new devil—one who isn't satisfied with simply claiming hell as his only domain.

The narrow unlit entrance beside the Scratchy Dog nightclub was not an alcove most women would find inviting but more like a place to be molested by some creep. At three o'clock in the morning on a Thursday morning, there weren't even drunk partiers to witness any nefarious activities. For Sere, however, the potentially dangerous doorway meant returning home—or as close to home as she hoped to find in New Orleans.

She pulled out her key, but as she touched the old brass handle, the door opened an inch on its own. *Shit*, she thought. The options of who might be lying in wait were almost too numerous to consider. At least the loas of the dead were not a possibility. They would have simply materialized in her room. And it probably wasn't another demon from hell. Joe and Bart had blasted the most recent batch into oblivion only four days before, and those doppelgänger escapees had needed three months to work their way out of hell and mount an attack.

Convinced that her intruder was human, Sere pulled the combat knife out of her boot. *I really need to figure out a way to carry my shotgun without being questioned by the cops every other block*, she thought. Not that she needed the four-barreled paranormal blaster against a human, but the weapon did make an impression. She edged the door open just far enough to silently squeeze in then eased it back in place. Only a small four-pane window at the second-floor landing illuminated the steep wooden staircase. She pressed her back to the dark wall and crept up the heavily painted steps. After six months of living in the loft, she'd mentally mapped out each creak and loose tread on the way to her sanctuary.

By the time she'd made it as far as the window, her eyes had fully adjusted to the dark. The door off the landing that led to the second floor of the Scratchy Dog had been sealed shut for decades. Just the same, she pressed her fingers against it to be sure no one was conducting a sneak attack on Kendell or Myles. She'd had more than enough of adversaries putting those she cared about at risk. The door didn't budge. At least whoever it was had the good sense to face her directly. That left out anyone from hell.

She kept below the window and continued up to her loft on the third floor. In front of a door covered in crackled ivory paint, she knelt in a runner's starting stance, careful to stay below the peephole. If anyone had made it into her apartment, her two canebrake rattlesnakes would hopefully either have them cornered or be waiting for her command.

She put her hand on the threshold, hoping to feel the gentle rattle that indicated they had the intruder under guard. *Nothing.* Her fingertips pressed the brass footplate. The door moved slightly against the latch but remained closed. *I still can't decide whether someone's attempting a sneak attack or trying to let me know they're here.*

Either way, confrontation was only the twist of a door handle away. She switched her handhold of the knife from slashing to throwing. She'd only get one shot.

She lunged off the ground like a frog, grabbed the top of the doorframe with her free hand, and kicked the door in. A shotgun blast from the middle of the room sent pellets into her hip, but most of the shot flew under her butt and into the angled roof above the stairs. Sere swung into the apartment, landed in a crouch, and flung the knife at Riley before the woman could recock her weapon. The knife penetrated deep into the woman's forearm.

Being a bartender, however, Riley was no stranger to fighting hurt. With her injured arm supporting the barrel, she pulled down on the trigger guard and brought the weapon up to her hip. "I'm not here to fight."

Sere lunged low over the floor, grasped the woman's legs, and dropped her like a sack of angry crawfish. The shotgun spun to the far wall. Sere's two snakes, who were supposed to be standing guard—or rather, slithering guard—fell from the rafters and wrapped their bodies around the weapon. While Riley was down and disoriented, Sere grabbed the knife out of the bartender's arm and stood over her. Blood dripped from the blade onto the woman's heart.

"You've got a strange way of asking for a meeting."

Riley pulled out from under Sere and cradled her bleeding arm. "Like you did Cody any better?"

At least the bar owner wasn't whining like a stuck pig. Despite being an ex-football player, Cody couldn't handle pain for shit. "That gator-hunting fool and I have a history," Sere said. "It was either stab him or be met with the demon he had hiding in his cabin."

Riley had the good sense to remain on the floor where she wasn't a threat. "We've got a history too."

Sere kept her aim on Riley. "Still, how difficult would it have been to make an appointment at Mr. Fisher's offices?"

Riley bent one of her long bare legs up, sending her cutoffs tighter up her ass. "You really are naïve, aren't you? Someone is always watching you, and not just the people you trust. The only way I could meet with you in secret was to break into your apartment. If those helping the swamp demons get wind that I met with you, they might get the wrong idea."

Sere wondered how much the woman knew about the demons' activities. If they did have accomplices among the living, though, she strongly doubted Riley would know about it. The woman was bluffing, but Sere decided to let her have her dignity. "I guess to stay in business, you side either with the denizens of hell or against them. But what the fuck are you doing here if it's not to settle the score?"

"Ram's been abducted."

Sere nearly dropped her knife in shock. "I just saw him yesterday—couldn't have been more than twelve hours ago. He brought by some police files."

"Well, he got a surprise when he got back to the bar. A

gang of your hell-based kin were waiting for him. They knocked him out and made their escape on the motorcycles they stole from the bikers. I hopped in my truck and hightailed it down here as soon as I heard."

Sere nearly swore out loud. The latest outbreak of demons had made it clear that they intended to kill her, but she honestly believed she had more time. "Why tell me? I'd think you'd be happy to lose the competition."

Riley pointed at the two of them. "You and I may have our disagreements, but I knew Rampart long before you showed up, and our history is a little more favorable, if you catch my drift."

Sere grimaced, trying hard not to envision Riley and Rampart naked together. Bart, as she liked to call him, had a way with women. From Riley's perpetually skimpy attire, Sere doubted it would have taken much manly skill to get the woman into the sack.

"What about his cousin Evert? Doesn't the parish sheriff's office do anything up there?"

Riley bent her muscular legs under herself and hopped back to her feet without changing her grasp on her wounded arm. "Do I look like someone the cops are going to listen to? I'm certain Ram's bar buddies filed a report, but I'm not optimistic about anyone doing anything. That police station runs on a skeleton crew at night. Anyway, it's going to take more than a deputy dude to find the demon bikers. As far as I'm concerned, until Ram's safe, I'm calling a truce between us. You're the best chance he has."

"A truce between us doesn't do me much good if all of your asshole gator-hunting customers are out to get me.

Last I heard, most of the Northshore is forming lynch mobs to go after the alligators that took out dozens of hunters, and I'm just sure everyone holds me responsible for organizing the attack. They probably got that idea from you."

Riley leaned against the wall. Blood covered her stomach, turning the waist of her skimpy white shorts dark red. "Can you blame them? You did come riding in from the swamp on that thirty-foot monster with a dozen of his prize-sized friends tailing you."

The woman had a point. All that Sere had accomplished by revealing the existence of Lefty, her gator friend from hell, was confirming to the hunters that there was something worth pursuing in the deep swamp.

"I was trying to warn them against hunting close to the hell mouth. In spite of the human casualties, the alligators were never the real problem. All those greedy bastards managed to do was provide their boats as transportation for the demons back to town. And you expect me to step back into that war zone? Bart's a big boy. He can take care of himself."

Riley wrapped what little there was of her cropped vintage-punk T-shirt around her arm. Her braless boobs pressed even harder against the stretched fabric. The faded image of Sid Vicious didn't look very dangerous as he stared at Riley's projecting nipple—more like a nerdy kid ogling his first breast.

"You're not fooling me," Riley said. "I know you've got a thing for that hot heroic hunk of man meat. The only thing you'd like better than being swept up into his arms is to be the one doing the rescuing."

Sere wondered if she was going to have to reevaluate Riley. The woman clearly understood her better than she'd realized. "Other than not filling me full of lead next time we meet, do you have any intention of helping?"

"I suppose I could run a commemorative-drink special for the gator hunters' fallen comrades. It wouldn't take a lot to get that posse so wasted they forget their mission. Of course, if you make it known you're up there, you're on your own."

"I'll take what I can get." Sere finally wiped her knife clean on her jeans and returned it to her boot. "I've got a med kit around here somewhere for our wounds."

Riley shook her head. "I'll be fine, and from what I've heard and seen firsthand, a couple of shotgun pellets in your ass aren't going to slow you down either. Mind telling your pets to let me have my gun back?"

One rattler coiled his body under the barrel like a spring. His head rested over the top like he was taking aim. His companion wound under the trigger guard like he was about to fire the weapon.

"They're free agents," Sere said, "and it looks like they want to hang onto your weapon. A snake never knows when he's going to need a little firepower."

I T WASN'T until the entry door downstairs slammed shut that Sere's two snakes slithered off of Riley's rifle.

"What the hell?" Sere yelled at them. "You two getting so fat and lazy hanging around Frenchmen Street eating big old rats every day you can't keep a scrawny barmaid out of my loft? If a girl can't trust her cold-blooded companions, who can she trust?"

They slinked toward the motorcycle bags on the bed as if the earlier shotgun blast had been the call to a new adventure. Sere grabbed her gun from the corner and tossed the saddlebags containing her reptilian friends over her shoulder. "I can't ride with these pellets in my ass, and wandering the streets, bleeding, is going to be a little conspicuous. But there's no point in wasting time making another trip to the loft." She checked her analogue wristwatch. "A little before four in the morning—Myles and Kendell should still be cleaning up downstairs. I suppose I should let them in on the latest disaster."

She hobbled down the two stories to the street. Adrenaline could carry her through the most intense battle, but without the natural drug, her body registered every ache and pain more than ever. *I really don't want to see Professor Yates again and have him confirm that there's something wrong with me.*

She kept her bleeding hip to the wall as she left her entrance and scooched open the door to the closed Scratchy Dog nightclub.

Kendell looked up from wiping down the bar. "Again? Please tell me this latest injury was just from you cleaning your gun." Kendell had stopped trying to offer sympathy for Sere's injuries, and Sere didn't understand that kind of talk anyway.

"I had a surprise visitor upstairs."

The club owner lifted the hinged section of counter. "Do I need to have Myles pull out the bleach and tarps?"

The couple hadn't yet needed to dispose of any doppelgänger bodies, since so far, no one had run across any of Sere's defeated opponents. "We settled our differences amicably this time. I just need a lift to the professor's lab for a quick body repair."

"You make it sound like you were in a fender bender." Kendell pulled at the side of Sere's jeans. "I'll have Myles bring the VW to the front. I swear, girl, you must never have to do laundry. Each time you get a new outfit, it invariably ends up shot full of holes, covered in blood, or stinking of swamp water."

Sere shrugged. "At least I don't have to worry about my wardrobe going out of style."

"Feel like telling me about your latest trouble, or are Myles and I just supposed to wait until all hell breaks loose again?"

"I'll tell you on the way."

At least explaining her situation to the couple meant Sere didn't have to face the new physical limitations that really worried her. She'd really hoped to put off meeting with the professor and Polly for a little while longer. But maybe with the others present, the scientist and his assistant would stick to healing Sere's latest injury and not get into the bigger problem of what was happening to her body.

9

2

*S*ere knew Polly was pissed from the way the woman locked eyes with her and didn't even glance at her damaged hip. "I'm guessing you're not angry at me because I woke you up at this ungodly hour," Sere said. "I'm sorry I didn't stop by earlier, but I haven't had a lot of time."

The former bandleader glanced around the professor's office. "I just thought you might prefer to deal with this in private."

Sere half sat on the end of the table to take the pressure off her hip. "I already know what you're going to tell me, so the only ones in the room who don't know are Myles and Kendell. Let me save you the trouble. Bart gave me a blood transfusion. He didn't have a choice as I'd lost a lot of blood and Jennifer was still in danger. I needed to heal as quickly as possible. So now I have a part of him in my doppelgänger body. I've been shot enough times to know the drill. You have to remove the foreign material before you can hook me up to Jennifer so I can draw on her energy. Blood, though, isn't something that can just be siphoned out of me. How am I doing so far?"

The professor nodded. His downcast eyes and tented fingers indicated the grave nature of her condition. "His blood contains human DNA."

"Right." Sere knew what was coming next—it was time to rip off the emotional bandage. "So I'm no longer immortal, but it's not that big a deal. If I'd lived a thousand years and now had to face a new mortality, I might be more freaked out. I just want to know if I'll live a normal amount of time or if there's some paranormal calculation based on the amount of his blood that's in me."

"What are you talking about?" Polly asked. Sere had expected the question, just not from the professor's assistant.

"Isn't that the big dark secret you wanted to tell me in private?" Sere asked. "Human DNA degrades, and Bart's is now a part of me. Ever since the transfusion, I've felt hunger, sleepiness, and increased pain. I never had to deal with these human conditions while purely Jennifer's projected doppelgänger."

The professor leaned back in his Barcalounger. "Polly, make a note: drama queen is apparently another side effect of human blood."

The woman glared at the old scientist. "Be nice. Can't you see how this has been eating at her?" She turned back to Sere. "Like it or not, you are still immortal. As you've noticed, however, the foreign body matter inside you has created some changes when it comes to projecting your real onto you. You're no longer strictly based on her existence. *That* was what I wanted to talk to you about before you leapt to conclusions. With the DNA as a guide for our projections, you'll be feeling more what it is to be human. You still don't need to eat or sleep. Naturally, our projection of Jennifer's body into hell and then through the gate to you will continue. You're still at least ninety percent doppelgänger. Having human blood in you isn't going to automatically give you a living body."

Sere wasn't sure how to feel. She considered being immortal the way a celebrity might think of being famous—it was a curse most people thought they wanted until it was actually theirs. If having Bart's blood inside her had somehow made her susceptible to his charms, she wasn't sure she'd be able to face him, which would be a problem when it came to his rescue.

"So other than having cravings, what can I expect?"

The professor brought up Sere's projection screen on his computer. "With your soul, you already experience a sense of identity independent of Jennifer Cranston. This latest development will probably create a similar distinction with her body." He turned away from his computer and pointed at her bleeding hip. "Which brings us to today. Since you're here, I assume you're on another save-all-humanity mission and can't wait to heal normally. Once we dig out the pellets, we'll hook you up as usual. The repair sequence shouldn't change, though it might take a little longer. However, what you experience inside Jennifer might."

"What about my situation with Bart?" Sere hated asking

the question, but if she was going to save the muscular bartender, she needed to be aware of any new vulnerabilities. To her relief, no one laughed at her or treated her like a teenager with a crush.

"Transferring bodily fluid isn't like sharing emotional energy," Professor Yates said. "It's not like he was psychically hooked up to you."

No, she thought, *but he did have his shirt around my neck with the technological bandage wrapped around it when he hooked me up to Jennifer. Combined with his blood in my veins, that had to have some effect.*

However, she didn't really want to argue that such a union was possible. With so much of her existence known and analyzed by the people in the room, having something personal was a rarity she chose to cherish rather than dig into. "Well, let's get this over with. I've got a bartender to save and some demons to kill."

SERE KEPT silent and tried to focus on nothing at all. Unfortunately, Jennifer was doing the same. The spatula in the woman's hand tilted, threatening to lose its grip on the hot chocolate-chip cookie.

Fuck. What new threat is this woman facing? Sere thought.

"I know you're there. I can feel you," Jennifer said in the empty kitchen.

Sere thought back over their last connection. *So long as I'm just thinking, she can't hear me.*

"Not talking? That's okay." Jennifer finished placing the

freshly baked cookie on the tray. "I'm not crazy. I know you were the one who saved Bobby, just like I knew you were the one who talked me through my rescue. How are those two sweet sticks of man candy, by the way?"

She's being way too calm about this. Damn it. How long does it take to heal a couple of shotgun holes, anyway?

"I'm just saying, you can talk to me. I won't freak out if that's what's worrying you. Bobby and Henry won't be up for another hour. I forgot I had to bake these for my son's class last night." She picked up one of the hot cookies and breathed in the smell of melted chocolate, butter, and nuts. "Tell me that doesn't smell good. I'll pour us some coffee so we can enjoy it together. All you have to do is say yes."

When did you become so damn good at manipulation? God, I hope some of me didn't transfer to you. Professor Yates had made it clear that if Sere kept messing around with his equipment while ignoring his fail-safes, such a possibility could happen, and nothing good would come of it. *Fuck it. This isn't going to be our last connection. I might as well get it over with.*

"Yes."

Jennifer's hand shook as she ran the spatula under the next cookie, crumbling it in half. "So you are there. I'm sorry about trying to trap you last time we met. That was unfair of me, but then, I guess we're both guilty of using each other."

Shit, woman, how much do you know? Sere didn't dare pursue her suspicions. She chose her words carefully. "We've helped each other out of some tough spots."

"That we have." Jennifer took a bite of the cookie and let the melted chocolate coat her mouth.

I'll have to reassess my opinion of your cooking. That's a damn fine cookie. Sere checked the corners of Jennifer's eyes to make sure there wasn't a package of frozen dough somewhere on the counter. "I never meant for this connection to happen."

Now, there was an understatement. If Sere's father hadn't yanked her out of Guinee and dumped her soul into the first little-girl doppelgänger he found, Jennifer would have had a perfectly normal life. The swig of coffee perfectly dissolved the chocolate in the woman's mouth into a rich, heady concoction that Sere wanted to take her time savoring, but it was gone before she could express her appreciation.

"Ever since I was a little girl," Jennifer said, "I've had an invisible playmate. I guess every child does at some point, but the feeling that there was someone else I could call on never went away."

I am not at your beck and call, Sere thought. "I hate to disappoint you, but sometimes—most of the time—the voices are just your imagination."

"But not always. That's good enough for me."

The tug indicating it was time to return to her body pulled at Sere's stomach. "Until next time. And thanks for the cookie."

$\mathcal{T}$he day was half-gone by the time Sere was back to fighting strength. "Where to next, demon huntress?" Myles asked as he opened the sliding door of the VW bus.

After a night of people and revelations, Sere was eager to get back on her Triton motorcycle, where she could think in peace. "Take me to Fisher's offices. I need to check in before grabbing my bike and heading out."

"And what can we do to help?" Kendell asked.

Kendell and Myles were as close to parents as anyone in Sere's life. She had left them out of the nightmare as long as she could—too long, Kendell would say. She needed to bring them back in.

"There has to be a way to close hell's gate to the demons without cutting off the connection that gives me this body," Sere said. "Since we can't get hold of Sanguine to find out what's happening on that side, we'll need to figure out how to slam the door on this side. I can hunt down these doppelbastards and behead them, but figuring out how they're getting through the gate is beyond me."

"What about your theory of one dead person killed by the existing doppelgängers equaling one new demon escaping hell?" Kendell asked from the passenger's seat.

"It's just an idea. Monty killed seven, then seven demons showed up three months later. I thought maybe there was some incubation period, but I must have been wrong on that point." She worried about what else she might have been wrong about. Being on the front line between life and hell meant everyone was relying on her for information and ideas. "From the police reports, those seven killed twelve gator hunters, so I'm working under the assumption that I'll be chasing twelve newly escaped demons."

"That's nineteen souls that could be trapped in hell," Myles said as he fired up the old bus. "We'll need to get them out before we seal the gate shut."

Kendell reached across the gearshift and touched Myles's arm. "Don't forget about Sanguine. I'm not just leaving her there to rot for all time."

Sere couldn't face leaving her guardian angel to hell's doppelgängers, but there were bigger considerations at the moment. "One other thing. The demons who abducted Jennifer were headed for the hell mouth. I'm worried they might have been trying to cast my real into hell."

"That's a lot of complicated," Myles said as he wove the VW into the early-morning traffic of the French Quarter.

For Sere, focusing on the specifics of how hell operated was a bit like being a kindergartener staring at a calculus formula. "You were the ones who asked for something to do."

"What about Joe?" Kendell asked.

Joe—Sere's mentor, trainer, and operations outfitter—would be her first stop after leaving the city. "Get word to him that I'm on my way. Don't leave anything out, including my new human DNA weaknesses. I'm not going to have many friends north of the city, so I'll need more than his advice this time. He might want to round up every paranormal shotgun shell he can find and grab a gun capable of firing them."

SERE BLEW RIGHT PAST LINDA, the receptionist, and into Montgomery Fisher's office. "We've got a problem."

The kindly CPA and superhero sidekick looked up from his stack of papers. "For the love of God, what now?"

She scribbled the address of Bubba's Bar and Grill on a scrap of paper. "Bart's been abducted by demons. They were waiting for him when he returned to Jackson's Bluff. Those doppelgängers can't resist a beer or two once they've escaped hell, so I'm guessing they rung up a healthy bar tab."

"You honestly believe they hung around to pay the bill once they abducted the bar owner?" Fisher asked.

Money never did make much sense to Sere. "Even if they did skip out without paying, eventually they will have had to refuel the motorcycles they stole. You worked some impressive financial magic last time to figure out the identities of the last doppelfuckers. Find me the direction these new hellholes are headed."

Fisher pushed his files aside and slid his laptop in front of him. "You think they'll be using bank cards?"

"All I know is they're more than a step ahead of me this time. It would have taken a small army to subdue Bart, so we're not looking at a lone demon finding his way in from the swamp like the last two times. Since they were coordinated enough to be waiting for him, it seems logical they would have arranged for the economic necessities before setting the ambush."

Fisher opened his cell phone. No matter which icon he pressed, nothing happened. The energy Sere projected had a way of screwing up wireless communication.

"I'll reach out to my bank contacts once you're out of the office." He half turned toward the corner of his office, where her backup single-barrel shotgun leaned at the ready. "What else do you need?"

"It'd be helpful if you didn't do anything stupid like putting your life at risk."

"Just following your lead. Is there any point in me rounding up Thomas? He might have some insight on what your latest band of demons are up to."

Fisher must have wanted a rematch with the professor's old assistant—demonically possessed to demonically possessed. Thomas had started it by abducting Sere and giving Fisher a concussion.

"I'm responsible for both of you having to share your bodies with your evil doppelgängers," Sere said. "Having you two try to kill each other again isn't going to help me find Bart."

"Fair enough." Fisher turned back to his desk and pointed at the computer screen that was still trying in vain to load the Internet. "Give me half an hour, and I'll have a direction for you."

SERE NEVER WAS much good at waiting for answers. Sticking around the office would only make the already gimpy French Quarter Internet connection move even slower. She headed out of the CPA's office to clear her head and stretch her legs. No matter which direction Fisher sent her, she was in for a long ride.

What she really wanted was a shot of Jameson, but she'd promised herself, as well as Bart, that she'd try to face reality sober for a while. As she passed out of the narrow business-lined street in the center of the Quarter, the gleaming marble facade of New Orleans Bank and Trust dominated her view. The fifteen-year-old structure had been designed to match the one Joe, Kendell, and Myles had bombed. Rubble from hell's version of the original two-hundred-year-old building had provided the material for the paranormal shotgun shells that could cut the link between a doppelgänger and its real.

But it wasn't the history of the demolished building

housing the interdimensional gate that made Sere stand with her fists at her sides. In the middle of the stone-slab-covered promenade that stretched out from the building's twelve-foot-high grand entrance was a new bronze statue of Baron Malveaux, complete with top hat and cane. "They just had to go and build you a goddamned monument."

"He did fund the construction of most of New Orleans after the War Between the States."

The voice behind her made Sere cringe. She turned to see a group of tourists reverently listening to a guide in a long coat and top hat. "A bit early in the day for such attire," she said. "Gentlemen didn't dress in tails unless they were attending a formal affair, and those were usually conducted after dark."

The tour guide bowed slightly. "Very good, my lady. However, after the war, it wasn't unusual for a fine gentleman to be left with a limited wardrobe." He spoke plaintively as if he himself had endured the hardship.

"Whatever." She turned back to the statue, grateful that at least the bronze remained silent.

The guide continued to address his crowd of families and hungover tourists. "As I was saying, as the head of the bank, Baron Malveaux had his hand in nearly every business transaction. The man was a true hero to the city. Most of what you see now was due to his generosity and savvy. Where others saw financial institutions in ruin, the baron saw opportunity. His lending practices were considered revolutionary at the time."

Sere really wanted to fight the arrogant prick. The expansive stone walkway would make for a wonderful field of combat. But she resisted her natural urges. Without turning away from the statue, she yelled, "His *practices*, as you call them, landed the women of most of the city's prominent families in his dens of prostitution. I'd hardly call that generous. The man was evil personified."

A gasp went up from the tourists behind her.

"Purely negative press," yelled the guide over his flock's rumbling. "Every failed business needed someone to blame, and the unfortunate baron bore most of the post-war animosity by those unable to capitalize on the city's rejuvenation. And unfortunate he was, for though he made and distributed his wealth to get the city back on its feet, his personal life was anything but enviable. His only son died in the war. His wife was committed to the care of the nuns—a discreet way of saying she lost her mind. And worst of all, his beloved daughter died from an evil curse."

Sere scuffled down the broad steps and away from the uneducated know-it-all before she lost her cool. *Now they're fucking using my life story to sell tours?*

She was still seething when she returned to Fisher's offices. "Tell me you've got something for me."

Fisher slid an old-fashioned folded map across his desk. "I called Bubba's Bar and Grill. As I assumed, they skipped out without paying for their drinks. However, Rampart Thibodaux's bank card was used at a Stop 'N Go outside Mason's Corner for ninety-two dollars' worth of gas. I don't imagine his Ducati holds anything near that amount."

Sere stared at the map. Mason's Corner was a good hundred miles north of Jackson's Bluff. "Damn it. They've got quite the head start. How long ago did they fill up?"

"Early this morning."

She unfolded the map to study a dot much closer to New Orleans. "What's this mark?"

Fisher took a Post-it Note off his desk phone and stuck it to the map. "Joe said to meet him at this address. He said he'd have everything ready to go."

4

*S*ere took the freeway exit to Myers, convinced that Joe was pulling a prank on her. The middle-class tract houses looked like something straight out of the 1980s. Rows and rows of nearly identical homes with practically the same conservative sedans parked out front made it impossible to differentiate the streets. As she consulted the small signs, she wondered how reality could be so damn boring compared to the make-believe existence she'd left in hell. She made a right onto Luther Lane and continued until she found the mailbox labeled 322. The dwelling looked exactly like the buildings on either side of it.

"Well, I guess that's one way to hide in plain sight." She got off her Triton and walked up the small incline to the front door. "I hope I don't scare the shit out of the occupants." After ringing the doorbell, she pulled her leather riding jacket tight around her bare midriff.

An old woman with a grandmotherly smile opened the door. "Can I help you, dear?"

Sere held up the Post-It as if it were some sort of pass to a hidden nightclub. "I was given this address, but there must be some mistake. I'm sorry to have bothered you."

Sere was just about to turn and leave when the woman said, "You're looking for Mr. Joseph, aren't you?"

"Is he here?" *This is some fucked-up hidden cache.*

"He rents the garage from me." The woman leaned out the door and pointed to the side of the house. "Just go through the gate. You'll see the side door to the garage. And tell him dinner is almost ready if he's hungry. That man never eats enough. There's plenty for both of you if you're hungry."

"Thank you." Sere walked away, genuinely confused by the woman's hospitality to a complete stranger.

As she pushed open the fence gate, a hand reached out and pulled her into the small alleyway. "Did anyone follow you?" Joe asked.

"How was anyone going to follow me? This is the most messed-up hiding spot ever. What the hell are you thinking, using a middle-class neighborhood to stash your weapons?"

He checked the street before closing the gate then rushed her into the garage. "I occasionally need a street address for deliveries and cover registrations."

"What the hell are you talking about?"

Once he had the garage door closed, he flipped on the lights. Other than his vintage BSA motorcycle in the corner and the two black-tarp-covered objects in the center of the concrete floor, the place looked deserted. He yanked the first tarp off, revealing a completely blacked-out motorcycle. "Honda Blackbird. This is one of the fastest production bikes on the market. She'll hit a top speed of one hundred ninety miles per hour." He pulled the covering off a second all-black bike. "BMW S1000 RR. Not a very elegant name for a superbike. She'll also do one ninety, but she's lighter and more maneuverable. I thought you'd find this one more comfortable. Since the demons abducted Bart, they'll be expecting you to chase them. That means they'll have a trap set for you. The way the rat avoids being killed is by moving faster than the spring after stealing the cheese."

Holy shit. Sere walked around the high-performance machines. "These bikes will make Bart's Ducati look like a moped."

"Our foe is a good eighteen hours ahead of us. Even on those lumbering Harleys, they'll have us at a disadvantage." Joe picked up the black helmet from under the BMW. "Try this on." He retrieved the matching one from under the Honda.

I hate full-face helmets, she thought, but she forced it over her head without complaining. "I can't see a damn thing."

"You can slide the screen up and out of the way if you want, but once you see what the computer display can do, you won't want to." She felt his hand press something under her chin. The screen lit up, displaying the room in shades of red with readouts too numerous to figure out.

"You realize this thing isn't going to do a damn bit of good out on the road, right?" Her energy had a way of fucking up anything not directly wired to what it was supposed to be reading.

"Maybe not." His words in her ears made her grip the sides of the helmet.

"What the hell, Joe?" She looked around for some connection between the two helmets.

"You've been working under a misconception. It's not that you can't use cellular technology. It's simply that your energy wavelength differs so much from what's currently in use that a distortion is created. You've been hooked up to the equipment in my cabin enough times for me to get a pretty good idea of what frequencies might work. I developed these helmets with Bart's help. That boy does know his covert communications."

She looked around the room with a renewed sense of awe. "So we'll be able to talk on the road?"

"More than that. Bart borrowed the technology in that helmet from fighter jets. You'll have readouts of practically everything you can imagine, including some that weren't part of the original military design." He touched a button under his helmet. His face instantly appeared on a little square in the corner of her view screen.

She looked at him past the readouts. His android-like black outfit meshed nicely with the color of the bike. "Are you saying we'll be able to identify the demons?"

"That's my hope. If they're on your energy wavelength, my modifications should help us zero in on their locations."

"What are we waiting for?"

He pointed at the package on the seat of the BMW. "There's a Kevlar riding suit for you. It's not as sexy as your leathers, but when you hit north of one hundred miles per hour, the wind can beat on your skin something awful. Just lose the riding jacket and shotgun, and the suit will fit over what you're wearing."

She looked at the closed garage door. "What about my weapons and saddlebags?"

He reached into the front cowling of the superbike. "I rigged up a couple of pump-action shotguns. All we'll need from your bags is your paranormal shells. I grabbed what I could from my cabin, but we can't be oversupplied with ammunition."

She hated the idea of leaving her snakes behind, but when it came to paramilitary actions, Joe was the boss. "That sweet little old lady I met at the door isn't going to object to a couple of snakes hanging out in her garage?"

She could see the snarky response beginning on his face in her view screen. "I'm sorry you won't be able to bring your teddy bears with you on this adventure. Madeline knows how to keep a secret."

"I deserved that. I suppose my snakes aren't much good against demons anyway." Sere wondered if the sweet-old-grandmother persona of the homeowner was just a cover identity. She was probably some spy Joe had worked with in the good old days.

He threw his leg over the Honda. "You always said you wanted to go on a covert operation with me."

"I get that these bikes are fast, but aren't they going to attract a lot of attention?"

He fired up his ride. Other than a soft continual huff, the bike was as quiet as a gator on the hunt. "The mufflers are fitted with silencers of my own design, and the black paint is military-grade radar resistant. The cops aren't going to notice us. With your helmet's night vision, you won't need the headlight unless you want to blind some oncoming vehicle. We'll be nothing more than wraiths in the night. Once I open the garage door, get your bike in here. Now that it's getting dark I want to cover as much distance as we can."

JOE KEPT his speed below eighty on the curvy swamp highway. Sere had grown fond of the Triton café racer she'd borrowed from Joe's cache near her swamp cabin. The BMW, however, was in a whole different category of motorcycle. At eighty miles per hour, the bike handled the curves like a swift diving for midges.

"How am I supposed to use this helmet if I don't dare take my hands off the controls?"

"Swipe your eyes across the screen like you're using a smart phone."

That made her ears cringe in frustration. "I don't fucking know how to use a smart phone." Her yell filled the small helmet.

"Sorry, my mistake. Look off to the side of the helmet. You'll see logos for the various functions. While staring at what you want, move your eyes back to the screen. The computer will do the rest. Ready to add a little throttle to these babies? I don't want them building up engine carbon from us reining them in for too long."

Excitement and fear were so close together in Sere's emotional catalogue that she wasn't sure which was making her heart beat so fast. "Let's do it."

Joe shot out in front of her as if someone had waved a starter's flag, leaving her standing still. She hunched down behind the small windscreen and opened up the throttle. Though the bike didn't make the roar of acceleration she thought it should, the backward pull to her body made her clamp her legs tighter to the gas tank. "Holy shit."

"Do I need to slow down?" His voice came through loud and clear even though he was little more than a red silhouette far down the road.

"Don't you dare," she said. His patronizing had the effect of bringing out her inner daredevil. She laid harder into the throttle, bringing the front tire off the pavement. "Last one to Bubba's Bar buys a round for the house."

The wind rushing over Sere's helmet drowned out the hush of the BMW engine. They were going one hundred miles per hour. On a long stretch of straight road, she held her body as balanced over the rocket as she could manage while keeping the small section of rubber tire in contact with the pavement, and she spun the throttle even further. And still Joe was pulling farther ahead.

"How the hell are you outrunning me? I feel like an airplane about to perform a liftoff." The speedometer on her visor read 113 miles per hour. The red dot far ahead that represented Joe read 126.

"Stop thinking and trust your instincts."

"I hope you've got a lot of paranormal bandage in that cowling in case I crash," she said.

"I thought you'd grown beyond that type of defeatist attitude."

She knew the argument well. Focusing on the worst-case scenario usually brought it into existence. Only by concentrating on what she wanted could she remain in control. She tucked her legs, arms, and torso even tighter to the high-powered machine and twisted the throttle until it wouldn't go any further. As she passed 120, control of the bike became more an extension of her thoughts than something she was operating. Instead of sliding off the roadway, she sliced into the curves like a figure skater carving up the ice with her blades. She breezed past a pickup truck as if it were a remote-control toy that had accidentally wandered into the roadway. Towns appeared on the horizon and faded out behind her without her ever noticing a single storefront. If a cop had noticed the blacked-out bikes, he didn't bother engaging in pursuit. And the motorcycle still had a higher gear.

By the time she realized they'd passed Riley's bar, Kelly's Diner was in her rearview monitor. *I've only got another twenty miles if I hope to pass Joe.* At least he was no longer putting more distance between them. *I know this stretch of highway well. This is my chance.*

The straight, smooth section of highway that the road crew had been laying when Sere had escaped Bart—what now felt like years ago—was finally paved though still coned off. In a split second, she made her decision. With a firm jerk to the BMW's handlebars, she jumped the bike over the uneven section of pavement and onto the fresh asphalt.

"That's cheating!" Joe yelled as she rocketed past him.

"You were the one who taught me to use every advantage."

SERE USED the entire length of the gravel parking lot to slide the BMW sideways to a halt. Joe was so close behind her that she could smell his brake dust. "Don't feel bad, old man. Even with my shortcut, if it hadn't been for my demon side, I'd never have beaten you. There were a couple of corners where I was certain I would go off the road and into the trees."

He pulled off his helmet, revealing his salt-and-pepper close-cut hair glistening with sweat. "I'll never complain about being beat by you, Sere. Let's see what these lost-biker dudes have to say about their missing bartender."

Her legs felt like they'd become a part of the motorcycle. Unwrapping them from around the curves of the gas tank was more intense than separating from a lover after sex. "Maybe you should go in first. Last time I was here, they weren't too happy to see me or my snakes."

He laid his helmet and gloves on the seat in the shape of a skull and crossbones. "Without their bikes and bartender, I suspect they'll be a bit subdued. Just the same..." He reached into his boot and pulled out a long thin knife. "Best to be prepared."

She patted the black handle sticking out of her gator-skin boot. "I'll follow your lead."

"That will be a first." He pushed his way through the

western-style swinging doors without waiting for her to respond.

Walking into the quiet dimly lit bar in their all-black riding suits made Sere feel as if she and Joe were the harbingers of doom. He continued on to the bar without giving the dozen forlorn men a second glance, but Sere knew he'd mapped out the establishment for threats and tactical advantages just as she had.

"Two ginger ales, a round for the house, and everything you know about the men who abducted your boss," Joe said.

The barmaid leaned over the cypress counter, displaying her cleavage clear down to the nipple-covering flowers of the lace camisole under her tied-off men's cotton shirt. "Sure I can't interest you in something stronger? You look like you could handle it."

Though Joe had the same woman-swooning charisma as Bart, at least the older man knew how to keep it in his pants. "What you have to tell me about Rampart should be plenty strong enough."

Sere pulled the knife out of her boot and placed it on the counter as she sat on the stool. "We know he's in trouble."

The woman finally turned away from Joe. "Oh, it's you. Didn't recognize you without your snakes or your shotgun. What is this, Take Your Father to Work Day?" The barmaid quickly turned back to Joe. "Not that you don't wear it well. Some men just naturally age to perfection."

Barf. Sere tried to contain her revulsion at the woman's outward display of lust. "Bart's in trouble, and you're wasting time, TT." *Tits and tips.* She smiled to herself at the inside joke that had spread about Bart's barmaid.

"It's *Edie*, if you don't mind. Ram might let you make up names for him, but I prefer my customers to be slightly more respectful. A woman has to stand her ground in a place like this."

Sere nodded her acceptance of Edie's chastisement. The woman had to have a strong spine to support those breasts —both physically and socially. "We both want the same thing—to save Rampart. Help us, and I'll make sure Joe becomes a regular."

The ex-Army Ranger leaned away from the bar. "The hell you will. I'm not just a pretty package, you know."

Edie pulled down a couple of glasses, filled them with ice, and squirted ginger ale into them from the bar's dispenser. "So long as I get a shot at displaying my skills." The way her eyes played over Joe's chest made it clear she wasn't talking about her mixology talents. "We typically get two groups of customers in here: those on their way home from work and those coming over after dinner. You can guess which group has the heavier drinkers. By six, the changeover is usually complete, and my day really begins. This group came in at about four and milled around the pool table. I could tell they were trouble. Do this job long enough, and it's not hard to figure out which customers are going to cause problems. I knew Ram was on his way, so I just tried to keep things civil until he got here. By the time my regulars had settled into their usual nightly routine around seven, the out-of-towners were good and sloshed and in no mood to hide it."

"How many were there?" Joe asked.

Edie looked over at the pool table as if trying to

remember. "Nine, ten—it's hard to be sure as they kept moving around."

"Could there have been twelve?" Sere asked.

"Maybe."

Fat Fuck, who never seemed to leave the end of the bar, squealed his stool as he turned away from his beer. "Closer to twenty. A dozen wouldn't have stood a chance against us." From his slurring, Sere guessed he'd been seeing double for days—probably well before the demons had shown up.

"Bullshit." Loud Mouth, at his usual table, appeared to have fully regained his voice after the busted jaw Sere had given him. "There were only seven of them."

"It took me all day to clean up this mess," Edie said incredulously. "Seven hoodlums couldn't have created that level of chaos."

"It's simple." Loud Mouth stood up as if preparing to give a lecture. "Seven of our Harleys were stolen, so there were seven in the gang."

"Some of them could have ridden double," Fat Fuck said.

Sere could tell she wasn't going to get a definitive answer. "What happened?"

"As I said," Edie continued, "I couldn't get an accurate count because they kept milling around, heading out for a smoke, using the can—basically, casing the joint. In hindsight, they must have been staking out the most strategic spots for when the action started. I'm sure you understand that better than I do." She raised an eyebrow at Joe.

You've got that right. Sere kept that thought to herself.

Being snarky would only waste precious time. "They were waiting for Bart?" she asked to cover her irritation.

"Apparently. We heard his bike pull up, but he never made it into the bar. I don't know how many they had outside to coldcock him, but there were enough of those assholes in here to keep my regulars occupied. It was bedlam—chairs, bottles, pool cues, blood everywhere. You have no idea what I had to go through to get this place open."

Loud Mouth put his empty glass on the bar. "I know enough about military tactics to recognize a collapsing defense when I see one. They kept fighting but only to confuse us. By the time the last one was out the door, the others had the motorcycles hot-wired. With all the crap all over the place, we didn't stand a chance of saving Ram."

Edie refreshed his drink. "You guys were falling all over yourselves, but you're right about the fight being planned ahead of time. I've seen a lot of bar brawls, but never one that well orchestrated."

Joe pushed his half-empty ginger ale toward Edie with two hundred-dollar bills under the glass. "What did they take? Which way did they go? And how far behind are we?"

Edie smiled as she slid one of the bills into her shirt next to her breast. "Eight motorcycles including Ram's Ducati. Lem and Kyle chased them north for ten miles, but that's not going to tell you much. The only intersections along the swamp highway lead to residential areas or hunting cabins." She checked the clock on the wall. "It's nine now, so they've got a good twenty hours on you."

5

*S*ere worked out the math in her head while Joe took point. *Twenty hours at, say, an average of fifty miles an hour puts them 1000 miles ahead of us. If we can average twice that speed, we'll have them by tomorrow evening—assuming Joe can last that long and we don't get pulled over. Shit. Better figure it will take twice that long.*

But instead of winding his motorcycle up to full speed, Joe hit the brakes and turned into the parking lot of an all-night diner at the edge of town.

"What the fuck, Joe?"

"We need a place to talk."

The light in Sere's helmet indicating that Joe was online switched off. She pulled so closely alongside his motorcycle that her foot hit his rear tire then reached behind her helmet and ripped it off her head. "The time to talk was back at Bubba's bar. This is the time to act. We're losing precious minutes."

He stepped off his bike and set his helmet and gloves down as if this wasn't going to be a quick stop. "The demons are *not* a thousand miles ahead of us. I'm getting a coffee." He walked to the door so casually that she wanted to throw her helmet at his back.

Instead, she set her riding gear down as he had and followed him to a booth at the back of the café. She scooched in toward the wall. "Explain, and don't leave out why we didn't have this discussion at our last stop—or better yet, on the road."

His look of cold disdain was one she knew well. Each time she failed one of his training sessions, silence was his initial response. "Think, little girl," he finally said. "Have I ever advised you to spill your secrets in a room full of strangers—and in a place you're known to frequent, no less? The demons were waiting for Bart. It's reasonable to assume someone was feeding them information. There could be a mole among the bikers or just some stranger happy to get a free beer in exchange for information, but the demons must have someone in this reality gathering information. But that's not why I stopped."

Being told she was being reckless didn't help with her desire to be back on the road. "They've got twenty hours on us, Joe. They could be clear across Texas by now."

He accepted the cup of coffee from the waitress. From her glazed expression, she didn't look to be paying attention to anything beyond the earbuds stuck in her head. "But they're not," Joe said.

"How do you know?"

"A fisherman doesn't pull his bait out so far from the fish

that she doesn't see it. He keeps it right in front of her mouth where she'll be constantly lunging for it. The demons are on this highway, and likely no more than ten or twenty miles down the road."

Sere sipped the hot coffee. It tasted like a combination of hickory and road tar. "They don't want Bart?"

"Of course not. He doesn't mean anything to them. He has no information, no money, nothing. They only took him to tempt you to the chase."

The coffee was slowly calming her doppelgänger side. "That's why they didn't simply kill everyone at the bar." Her tactical analysis started kicking in. "If they had, Bart would have fought to the death for his buddies. So if they haven't been running, they've had all that time to build their traps for us."

"Probably, but that's not all of it. What else did we learn?"

She felt like a little girl sitting in the Scratchy Dog while Joe taught her military tactics. "They hid their numbers, but that could have been simply to keep Bart off guard."

"The Navy SEAL is good, but taking on any more than half a dozen demons singlehandedly would be suicide. For a moment, let's go with Edie's low end of nine doppelgängers and your theory of one dead to one demon. That last batch of hell's escapees killed twelve before we put them down."

Sere's heart began a firm rapid pounding. "That would leave three unaccounted for. They could be following us as the back door to the trap. Once we're in the demons' kill zone, they could cut off our escape."

Joe sipped his coffee. "Possibly, but even against nine

41

demons, the two of us would be badly outnumbered, especially with them in control of the war zone. They don't really need all twelve."

Sere set the coffee cup down and stared into Joe's eyes. "You think those three are headed to New Orleans, don't you?"

"Their ultimate prize, at least according to you, would be to take over the lives of their reals. Say you're right about an adversary in hell working on getting his demon horde into the land of the living. He's already proven that they can escape hell. What would be his next question?"

She began to see where Joe's logic was headed. "He wouldn't know if a doppelgänger killing his real would result in a stable life for the demon. This breakaway force might be an attempt to test that theory. In which case, the chase we're on to save Bart is nothing more than a diversion to keep me out of the picture. But what choice do I have? If we don't save him, they'll kill him just to spite me." Sere couldn't let that happen. She balled her hand into a fist next to her coffee cup, once again wishing they were on the road.

"Who do you trust to take point in New Orleans? We need to know for sure if there are demons headed that way."

She forced her hand open and took another sip of the coffee. "Montgomery Fisher. He likes to joke that he's my superhero sidekick. Kendell and the others would rather muck about with their science experiment, and that's not going to save anyone in this realm. As a CPA, Fisher had the contacts that led us to the last gang of seven demons and pointed me in this direction. He can be a bit impetuous, though."

"He'd have to be to follow you. I'll get word to him of our suspicions. If he can identify the demons and get eyes on their reals, that'll put us one step ahead when we get back to the city."

But three demon steps behind. Once again, Sere felt like they were wasting time. "What are you expecting in terms of the trap we'll be rolling into?"

"I go into battle prepared for anything but free of expectations." He pushed his empty coffee cup aside. "You take point this time. Keep your speed to sixty. We want to have the punch to get away, but first, we'll need to spring the trap."

AT SIXTY MILES PER HOUR, the BMW felt like a harnessed greyhound straining at his leash. "I feel like a sitting duck out here," Sere said.

"That's the point. Keep off the com and stay focused, but don't just rely on the technology in front of your eyes. You're based on the same stuff as our adversaries, making you our best indicator of their location."

So what's the point of all this bullshit in front of my face? With the display already in shades of red, Sere found it hard to tell when her irritation was allowing her demon side to kick in. "What do I do once I spot one?"

"If they're on their motorcycles, lay into the gas and get in front of them. I'll hang back and pick off what I can. Those Harleys won't be able to manage much more than sixty on these curvy roads. Once you've got a little space in front of them, circle back. The hardest thing to attack is something attacking you—in humans, it causes a defense mentality to kick in. We need to reduce their numbers before they can mount a counterattack."

"And if they've set an ambush?"

"Wait until they show their hand. Once they attack, get the hell out of there. That's what the bike is for. They're not going to risk losing sight of you. As soon as they give chase, I'll start picking them off from the rear."

After ten miles of creeping around each corner like a little girl afraid of turning into a dark hallway, Sere was tired of playing the victim waiting for her attacker. "Come and get me, assholes."

She twisted the throttle, shooting the bike from a leisurely sixty miles per hour to one hundred twenty in the blink of an eye. The small display in the bottom right corner of her visor showed she had left Joe in her dust. *Faster. Go faster.* The desire was inescapable. As she set up for a hard right corner, the digital readout displayed a flashing 136 miles per hour.

An explosion under her ass blew out the tire just as she leaned into the curve. Instead of hunching over the bike as it hung onto the speed-demon corner with all of its g-force, Sere sailed straight off the road, over the trees on the embankment down to the water, and fifty feet out into the swamp. The screeching of metal meeting tree trunk behind her announced the end of the beautifully dangerous BMW just before the explosion lit up the night sky. *Joe is going to kill me.*

6

"**W**hat happened?" Sere tried moving, only to find her arms and legs bound behind her like a stuck pig.

"My guess is you were acting recklessly again."

The sound of Bart's voice made her roll over on the wood-plank floor. He sat against the wall, buck naked, with his wrists and ankles tied together in front of him.

With a little undulating, she realized she too had been deprived of her clothes. "They didn't leave much to chance, did they?" Looking around the room, she couldn't find a stick of furniture, a picture frame on the wall, or even a pane of glass in the boarded-up windows.

"Apparently, our reputations extend all the way to hell," Bart said. "How are you feeling?"

Everything hurt. She ran her analyses out loud so she wouldn't have to deal with the individual pains twice. "My brain is fuzzy as hell. I must have a concussion, but I'm conscious, so it can't be too bad." Her right arm was securely tied, but her left arm moved a little too easily against the binding—just in the wrong directions. "Dislocated left shoulder and broken forearm." Breathing hurt, making it impossible to lie on her left side. "At least three cracked ribs, but I don't think they're broken. The pain is sharp, but I'm not tasting blood." She pulled her ankles under her butt and managed an upright, if totally undignified, position. "Legs are fine. I must have landed headfirst on my left side."

"Good thing you've got a hard head. What are we looking at timewise for you to heal?"

With a psychic shot of Jennifer's soul, the regeneration might take a few hours to get back to full strength, but out in some abandoned shack in the swamp, that wasn't going to be possible. "The greater the damage, the longer it takes," Sere said. "Without a little paranormal help, I'd guess three days for the internal breaks to mend. Sleep might cut that number in half, but this isn't exactly a relaxing situation."

"Damn. Sounds like we're screwed."

At least Bart had the good sense not to ask about Joe. Sere had no way of knowing who might be listening outside the door. She closed her eyes and tried not to focus on her body's pain. *If those doppelholes are anywhere nearby, I should be able to detect them.* After thirty seconds she opened her eyes and grunted in exacerbation. "Professor Yates is so full of shit."

"I take it you're not detecting anything from the demons," Bart said.

"I'm hurt, wet from being in the swamp, tired, and cold. So yeah. Nothing."

Much as she didn't want to admit it, she couldn't get her mind off the fact that they were locked alone together, naked. He extended his legs as far as his bound wrists would allow then scooted his butt off of the wall. As she watched him struggle toward her, she hoped there weren't any rough boards to give him splinters in his muscular ass—or worse, an even more sensitive part of his body.

"What are you doing?"

He snuggled against her side. "I can't do anything about your injuries, dry you off, or give you my energy, but at the very least, I can help warm you up."

Her body melted against his. She rested her head on his shoulder. "I really fucked things up, didn't I?"

"I've seen better rescues, but then, I've also participated in worse. Try to get some rest. Anything we can do to get you back into fighting shape is a good thing."

SERE COULDN'T IMAGINE what alien reality she'd landed in this time. Falling asleep was like playing spin the bottle with hooded suitors. Removing the covering could reveal anything from new incantations of hell to an unimaginable nirvana. Whoever's life she'd landed in was completely fixated on the half-empty bottle of Jamaican rum. *Blech. Who could drink that sweet shit?*

"You gonna help me clean up this mess or what?" a voice asked.

The eyes finally pulled away from the caramel-colored luscious liquid to the scantily clad waitress standing in the middle of the busted-up bar. *TT? What the hell? I'm in fucking Bart!*

"She was really something, don't you think?" the bartender slurred.

"No. I think she was a scrawny-ass bitch who got into a bar brawl about nothing. Come on, boss. Put the bottle away. We both know you don't need it."

"Need, want—what's the difference?"

Edie leaned the broom against a broken chair, walked up to the bar, and spread her hands on the counter wide enough to highlight her breasts. "You're better than this. You can have any woman within a hundred miles of this bar. If you doubt me, just say a name, and I'll bring her here to prove it. That motorcycle-riding witch is not worth it."

This must be after we first met. I had no idea I'd left such an impression on him, Sere thought.

He set the bottle on the shelf behind the bar. "But not one of them could handle herself in a fight."

In the bar mirror, Edie stood up straight and put her fists on her hips. "Excuse me. Who just busted Leroy over the head with a beer bottle? I can handle my own—and yours too if you'd give me half a chance."

He turned around and traced every curve of her well-endowed body with his eyes. "Tempting, Edie. Very tempting. But you remember our agreement. No fucking around with coworkers, and that includes you trying to seduce the boss."

Edie bent her head back, sending her platinum-blond

hair cascading over her bare shoulders and thrusting her breasts forward under her strapless crop top like torpedoes about to fire out of their tubes. "You don't want me? That's fine. I'll go get Riley. You two have been fuck-buddies for as long as I can remember. A night of destroying bedroom furniture usually makes you feel better."

He grabbed a rag and started sweeping the broken glass from the bar into a large garbage can. "You've made your point."

"She's not even your type. Skinny, short hair, no boobs to speak of—any other night of the week, you wouldn't have given her a second glance. Hell, I'd have had to wait on her myself."

"I said drop it, Edie."

"Not until you tell me why she has you so spun up. I've never before seen you act like some little boy who's scared of girls."

He could tell her to fuck off. He wanted to. She was his employee, and though he gave her a lot of leeway due to her popularity with his customers, casting aspersions on his masculinity wasn't something he could accept. *Fuck it*, he thought.

"Scared? I don't think so." He tossed the rag into a bucket by his feet and unlatched his belt buckle. "Strip naked and bend that round ass over the bar right now, little lady."

SERE WOKE up in a cold sweat. Witnessing Bart hammer his cock into his waitress wasn't her idea of a restful sleep.

Once the pair had started going at it, however, it seemed rude to leave. Nothing about the encounter carried any emotion other than a release of frustration. And she'd caught Bart imagining he was fucking her and not the waitress through the haze of endorphins.

She leaned away from his sleeping naked body. A white sticky substance coated her hip where it had come to rest close to his lap. *Not how I envisioned our first sexual encounter.*

"How do you feel?" he asked while keeping his eyes closed.

Shit. "I thought you were still asleep."

"I was until you moved off of me."

Sere flexed her left arm and took a deep breath. *All healed.* Between the blood transfusion he'd given her and his shirt wrapped under the paranormal bandage when he'd conducted her healing while saving Jennifer, she and Bart must have established a usable connection. To heal her so quickly, the power supply had to be as intense as the man himself.

"Much better after my nap. How about you?"

"I had the strangest dream about when we first met," he said.

She rubbed her arm against her hip to get rid of the evidence. *God, I hope he doesn't notice.* She wanted to get him onto another topic before he fully woke up. "What can we expect from our abductors?"

Bart pulled his body into a tight crouch. "I'm a bit surprised we haven't seen them yet. Something must have distracted them."

She could only hope Joe hadn't gotten himself killed

trying to save her. "Give me the tactical rundown of what happened."

"When I got back to the bar, I barely made it off my Ducati. The moment I took off my helmet, something struck me hard on the back of the head. I was gagged and hogtied to the back of my bike before I regained consciousness. When I came to, the leader was holding my evasion knife to my face. He said if I behaved, they wouldn't kill everyone in my bar. I've been around you long enough to know the demon wasn't bluffing."

"Joe figured they must have offered the lives of your customers in exchange for your cooperation," Sere said, deciding that if her mentor was the one distracting the demons, there wasn't much reason to keep his involvement a secret from Bart.

"I'll bet he told you to take it easy on the road too, didn't he? You must have expected a trap. What the hell were you thinking?"

Her irritation helped distract her from the emotional connection she couldn't shake. "Do you always get in fights with those debriefing you?"

"God, I could use a drink right now." He closed his eyes and took a few slow, deep breaths. "There were nine of them. So far, the only one who's said anything is their leader. This is a much more disciplined and organized group than those last idiots. Once they dragged me to this cabin, they stripped me naked. I'm guessing that was to discourage me from escaping as well as to make sure I didn't have anything I could use. They've left me alone until they dumped you in here with me."

"They probably stripped you so they would be free to come after me."

"That was my assessment as well. So long as all nine of them were hanging around the cabin, I didn't stand much of a chance at attacking, but if they intended on only leaving a small guard force, they'd want me as docile as possible."

Sere twisted her left wrist against the rope. When they had tied her, they must have known about the dislocated shoulder and busted bone. They left just enough play in the rope for the slack line to snag on a nail head. She locked eyes with Bart and nodded toward her back.

He returned her nod and got down on his side.

This is going to be embarrassing. Like I needed more reason to blush. She turned away from him and shifted her tied wrists and ankles close to his mouth and hands. His hot breath on her butt cheeks made her quiver.

The door burst open before Bart could loosen the knots with his teeth. "I think that'll about do it for the escape attempt," the intruder said. "Though I am curious to see what kind of mischief you two would get into once you were free of your bonds." The demon held a charred shotgun at Sere's head. She hoped it was the gun from her motorcycle and not one they'd taken off Joe.

"You won't kill me," she said. "You've had plenty of chances. Even without the magic bullets in that shotgun, all you would have needed to do is lop off my head with one of Bart's knives."

He lowered the weapon. "I'm not here to kill you. Not yet at least. For the time being, we need you. Your connection to hell is like a high-voltage power line, and we're the neon tubes being lit up just by being around you."

"You have to be fucking kidding me. *I'm* the reason you can exist here?" Sere began to wish he had shot her. At least then, those she cared about wouldn't be put at risk.

"That's the theory. I'd have thought someone on this side would have already figured that out."

She silently swore at Professor Yates. Either he knew of her connection to the demons and kept it from her, or he wasn't nearly as smart as he believed. "So if you don't plan on killing me, why go to all the trouble of enticing me out here?"

"Think of me as hell's technician. The real genius is back in that realm, working up his experiments. I'm here to conduct the tests."

In her opinion, there was nothing worse than a demonic science geek. "And you expect me to just go along like some kind of lab rat?"

"Your obvious resistance is why we've got you stripped and tied. Like the lab rat, we're not giving you a choice."

Sere always had a choice, but challenging him while defenseless didn't seem the brightest move. "At least let Bart go. He's not a part of this."

"Oh, he's very much a part of this," the demon said. "You care about him. That emotional connection is what holds you to this life. He's like the power tower that supports the high-voltage line. We thought it was Jennifer, but it turns out you're just using her."

Sere couldn't turn toward Bart. The demon was right

but not entirely. Bart was one of many that she cared about. "What's the first test your evil master has planned for me?"

The demon ejected one of the shotgun shells and rolled it menacingly between his fingers. "I would have thought that was obvious." He squeezed one of the pellets out of the casing. "Now, swallow the pill like a good little doppelgirl." He cocked the weapon and aimed it at Bart. "Or your friend gets the full blast, and unlike you, he can't regenerate."

"You'd cut my connection to my real to study the power cable? That doesn't make any sense. If you are feeding off of me, you'll just be hurting yourself." She hoped questioning him might buy a little time. *Come on, Joe, get your ass in gear and save us.*

"Not the whole connection, just a temporary slice out of a single strand."

"Don't do it, Sere." Bart struggled against his ropes as if anger alone could burn them from his wrists. The move positioned him over the nail head that had been under her ass.

She stared into his eyes. "It'll be okay. I'll come back to you."

7

*U*nlike waking up in a dream state in hell, spiraling through the power connection felt like being falling-down drunk. Every part of life that she tried to hang onto slipped through her mental grasp. *At least I'm not feeling any bodily disintegration. It's just my immortal soul that's in danger.*

When the whirlwind of perceptions died down, Sere was inside a small room made of iron walls like the cabin of a submarine. The shelves bolted to the sides were filled with wooden boxes. She pulled her arms around her stomach as the reality of where she stood took hold. "I know this place."

"It's where you were created."

Sere turned around at the sound of the woman's voice. Behind her was her hell's angel, Sanguine Delarosa, granddaughter of hell's creator and coconspirator in casting Sere's father into the dimensional dungeon.

Sere didn't know if she should be happy to see Sanguine,

pissed that the woman hadn't been doing her job of containing the demons, or concerned that the box where she'd been created might also be where she would have her soul permanently removed from her doppelgänger body. The overload of emotions caused her to resort to the logic-based computer-controlled doppelgänger she'd left in life.

"So this is why you haven't stopped the demon horde?"

Sanguine's once pure-white wings had turned yellow like the feathers made from old paper. "Nice to see you too. You barely made it through the gate when I was taken. What are you doing back here?"

Sere looked around the cramped room in frustration. "I'm afraid I'm not faring much better than you are. Some demon from this side is playing mad scientist, and I'm the lab rat. He's been sending groups of doppelgängers across. This latest batch is apparently trying to figure out how I'm connected to hell." Sere limited how much information she shared. Joe had already chastised her once for almost saying too much in a room controlled by the enemy.

Sanguine pulled down one of the wooden boxes. "I'm not completely oblivious to what's going on." She opened it. Inside was the cursed pipe tool Sere had used to cut her wrists nearly two hundred years earlier. "If I hold it long enough, I can get mental flashes of what you're doing."

"So the demons think that with you and *that thing* in here, they can control me?"

Sanguine closed the box and put it back on the shelf. "You just said your troublemaker is a mad scientist. One of the first things he'd do is limit the variables to his experiment."

Sere suspected the demon technician also wanted her to see the power he was holding over her. With more than one pellet in her, she'd have been stuck in the vault like a magnet to all of the cursed items and her power-supplying angel. "What other good news have you got for me?" she asked sarcastically.

"Whoever is responsible for abducting me and sticking me in this cage had to know of your history. At the time of your creation, all the people in this realm, other than you and I, were mindless doppelgängers copying the actions of their reals."

A cold chill went up Sere's back. "What are you thinking?"

"The power leading this assault on us is from the land of the living."

Sere held her arms even tighter around her stomach. "Someone in life is raising an army of the damned?"

"If they are, they're doing a pretty piss-poor job of it. You keep sending the demons back the way they came like naughty little children you caught running away from home. You're going to have to do better than assume someone's simply out to get you."

Sere wondered how many demons her adversary would have to send before she understood their plan. "I don't get it. I can see why the doppelfuckers want to escape hell and take over the lives of their reals. They're not happy that I'm standing in their way. And the demon technician made no secret of the fact that hell was trying to figure out how I power the escapees. But why would anyone in *life* care?"

"I asked myself the same question." Sanguine reached

out to touch Sere's arm, but the hand fell through the empty air of her soul. "All I know is they are specifically after you."

"You think maybe the loas of the dead convinced someone to do their dirty work?" Sere knew the loa-holes had done something similar in convincing Myles to deal with her father.

"They don't know you're among the living. Even if they did, using denizens from another dimension isn't how they roll."

Sere knew that the loas of the dead had powerful resources, and so far, at least the voodoo community had been staying out of the demon outbreaks. "That would just leave those close to Aunt Kendell, but if it was someone like the professor feeding hell information, they wouldn't need to be running tests on me. The professor knows pretty much all there is to know about how I'm kept alive."

"There is one other person who knew more than anyone about how you were created, though."

The chill in the room seemed to intensify. "You told me years ago that he's gone, never to return."

"Myles and Kendell assured me your father's spirit is resting in the *deep waters*. I have no reason to doubt them, but Baron Malveaux did create you. He was no dummy. He would have kept records of what he was doing in case there was a problem or to allow him to reproduce his success." Sanguine motioned around the room. "And none of his journals are among his cursed possessions."

"Even if the records aren't in this room, the lab books would still be in hell, not among the living."

Whoever was directing the demon technician, however, probably had access to the information. Sere felt as if every aspect of her existence had just been laid bare to some creepy stalker. And she feared Sanguine was right—no doppelgänger in hell had the mental capacity to be the one in charge.

"I'm afraid being stuck in this box has its limitations," Sanguine said. "I've had way too much time to think with no ability to test or research my theories. I'm no expert on the paranormal science that keeps you alive, so I wouldn't even know where to look. Of everyone, I trust Kendell the most, but I'd advise not telling her of my suspicion that someone on the side of the living is responsible until you have more facts. If it is someone close to her, she'd never be able to keep it secret. Whoever is after you would have to have influence both among the living and in hell."

Sere had never needed Sanguine by her side more than she did at that moment. "How do we get you out of here?"

"I don't even know where *here* is. This interdimensional vault was a bugger to break into when the devil held Kendell captive in it. You have bigger problems than freeing me. Now, how do we reverse this experiment they're running on you?"

"The demon only forced me to swallow one pellet. Now that I've adjusted to it, I can feel the current that flows between this box and life. Bart's on the other side. Our connection is stronger than that demon suspects. If I focus on that union, I should be able to pull myself out like I was hauling on a lifeline."

Sanguine's raised eyebrows suggested that she wanted to

ask about this unexpected love development, but she only said, "Play your cards close to your chest."

Sere wanted to comfort her beloved angel. "I know how to find you now. Once I stop this demon uprising, I'll be back to save you."

∾

SERE'S AWARENESS of being in the cabin in the swamp returned as someone slapped her in the face. "You back?" The demon bent over her like a schoolyard bully.

She leaned hard against Bart. "What'd I miss?"

"He got pretty woozy," Bart said. "His skin glistened transparent."

"That's enough," the demon said. "We tried turning the dial down. What say we ramp things up and see what happens?" He held up a technological bandage.

Sere strained against the ropes. "Where the hell did you get that?"

"If you wanted to keep your healing technology a secret, you shouldn't have left it sitting in that abandoned school bus. We might not understand how it works yet, but when your soul was powered up into another human, my brothers received the hyped energy. Tracing the source to the bus in the swamp wasn't really that difficult."

Sere considered the explanation pretty thin and too well rehearsed. If she couldn't detect the demons, she strongly doubted any of them could feel her either. With Myles standing on the roof of the bus to establish the remote connection to the professor's equipment, anyone could have seen what the gang was up to. So many people had been present when Sere came out of Jennifer, after saving her from the demons, that it had been damn near a hell-guardian reunion in Joe's school bus cache. Sanguine must have been right. There had to be someone working with the demons.

"First, we need a reason for you to draw on your real's energy." The demon pulled her combat knife out from the back of his pants. The blade gleamed in the swamp moonlight. He lifted it to his shoulder and made a backhanded downward slash toward her chest.

Before the blade could make contact, however, Bart jumped up from the floor, grabbed the demon's extended arm, and flipped the doppelfucker to the ground. With a firm karate kick, he crushed the larynx in the sickly-looking neck and kept the demon from crying out. Bart nearly pulled the transparent hand off the wrist as he took the knife. Then with one savage swing, he sliced the demon's neck to the bone. Finally, Bart lifted his foot from the demon's chin and slammed his heel into the exposed vertebrae as if stomping the life out of a partially decapitated rat in a trap. With a backward kick, he sent the head flying halfway into the room.

Instead of coming over to free Sere, Bart rushed to the shotgun in the corner of the cabin. He motioned for her to stay silent.

"Russ, you in here?" a voice yelled from outside. "The mosquitoes out here are eating me to death. There's no one coming."

Bart took aim at the side of the closed door.

"I hope you're about done with your test. She made me all woozy. I'm coming in to get something to drink." Doppelidiot number two stumbled into the cabin like a drunk while holding Bart's handgun at his side.

With one clean shot, Bart filled the demon's head with paranormal pellets. He then gave the pump-action shotgun a firm pull and let a second round follow the first. The denizen of hell disintegrated completely without ever lifting the handgun.

"Interesting," Bart said. "I've never seen one completely evaporate before. Even out in the swamp, the gators got to them before I could finish the job."

"Yeah," Sere said. "If the connection is fully severed, there's nothing left of them in this realm. Now, if you don't mind, being tied up naked isn't my idea of sexy. I'm more the tie-others-up kind of girl."

He kept the hold of the shotgun and grabbed the knife from the floor. "I can see that about you."

Sere rolled to her side so he could cut her loose. "That was a pretty impressive rescue. I assume you used the nail head to loosen your bonds. How long did you have to wait after you were free of your ropes?"

Once her bonds were cut, he handed her the knife as if she might feel less naked and vulnerable while holding the weapon. "Too long. I didn't want to attack until I knew you were back in your body. When I saw him holding the bandage, I knew he'd be coming in close and that would be my best shot."

She got to her feet. Everything hurt. "It's a good thing you did. If he'd wrapped that cloth around me and turned it on, the shotgun pellet could have bounced around inside me like a pinball before exiting my body. With its disruptive energy, I could have been left with a permanent hole in me."

"Don't fancy a whole-body piercing?" Bart joked. "I doubt he even knew how to use that bandage." He snuck back to the door and peered out the crack. "We need to get out of here. How are you feeling?"

Resisting the pull toward hell was like standing in a river, holding firm against the current, and Bart was the rock she was using for stability. "Just stick close to me."

"We'd better hurry. Grab the handgun. There were only those two when they dropped you off, which means there's seven more demons out there somewhere. Joe is good, but even he can't keep them distracted forever."

And three more in New Orleans testing out immortality, she thought. *One nightmare at a time.* Sere kept close behind Bart as he opened the cabin door and snuck outside holding the shotgun.

"Mind watching where you stick that knife?" he said.

"Sorry." She lifted the sharp blade from beside his butt cheek to her chest. "Any idea where the road is?"

"Can't be far. My best guess is it was about twenty minutes between the explosion and when they had you stripped, tied, and dumped in the cabin. But their legs were wet from fishing you out of the swamp, and I didn't hear a motorboat, so there has to be a trail around here somewhere."

She pointed to the piles of clothing where their second guard had been keeping watch. "First things first."

8

The Kevlar suit was trash, but it had done its job well. Sere's leather pants, cropped leather top, and holster were unscathed. Once again clothed, with her weapons where they belonged, she followed Bart along the path that led away from the cabin.

"Where do you think Joe is?" she asked.

"I can just make out a faint glow through the trees. Must be what's left of the BMW. If I were him, I'd work my way into the dark of the swamp and keep the demons between me and the light. That would give him the best advantage for seeing the bastards."

Bart had stashed his gun in the back of his pants and carried one of his many knives. With only demons to fight, a conventional bullet would only slow them down, but cutting off their heads would be a permanent solution. Sere fondled the butt of the pump-action shotgun, which barely fit in her thigh holster. The paranormal shells in it were their best weapon against the demons, even though carrying the rifle as they hunted through the swamp interfered with her maneuverability.

"So we work around the shoreline, searching for him?" Sere knew fighting well, but she left military tactics to the expert.

Bart hunkered down beside a tree stump. "We can do more damage to the enemy if we remain separate. Joe and I have similar training, so he'll be expecting me to create a second offensive. Once he knows you're free from the demons, the fun will really start."

"Sounds like a lot of assumptions. Why wouldn't he just keep riding after the crash to spread out the doppelfuckers?"

Bart looked at her as if she were a stupid little girl. "For starters, he'd want to make sure you weren't killed. That means stopping somewhere. Riding up to the crash scene would have put him in the enemy's crosshairs. The instant he heard the explosion, he probably pulled off the road in order to stay hidden and check that you weren't followed. With any luck, the demons didn't realize he was with you, though a squad with any training at all would conduct a search to be sure you were alone. Between your abduction after the crash and your time as their guinea pig, Joe has had an hour or so to play sniper games with the demons. We already figured something distracted them from showing up at the cabin. Since we escaped without running into another contingent, I think it's safe to say Joe is out here somewhere."

Sere looked back toward the road. "So which way do we go?"

Bart pointed down river. "Toward where he would have left his motorcycle."

An ugly thought crossed Sere's mind. "I hope you're not proposing that I make a run for it while you two play commandos with the demons."

"That's not what I'm suggesting, but it probably is the escape Joe set up for you. I don't think he would expect you to take it unless you had to. We can use the bike as a distraction to give him the upper hand with whoever he might be chasing. Even if they don't want you dead, when the demons see you standing on the highway, they'll come after you. Our elevated position with Joe out in the swamp should put the demons in a good kill zone—assuming they haven't captured him. Stay sharp. Our enemy will have stationed lookouts between the road and the river in case we broke free."

She desperately wanted to take the lead. The swamp was her home. Doppelgängers from hell would be completely out of their comfort zone, making them easy to spot. All she had to do was watch how the animals responded. But if something happened to Bart without her knowing, her soul might get swept back to hell.

"You take point," she said. "I'll be right behind you."

He gave her a quizzical smile. "You sure?"

Knowing that she couldn't hide their connection forever, Sere decided to fill him in. "When you gave me that blood transfusion, we established a bond. Then when you powered me up with your shirt under the bandage, you made it more than just physical. With this pellet in me, I need your soul to hang onto so I don't slip back to hell. Sorry to lay this on you, big boy, but for now, you're my rock."

"I'm not sure if I'm supposed to be honored, apologetic, or turned on. Clearly, though, this is a conversation for another time." He looked out at the dark vegetation. "We can't wander through the swamp joined at the hip. Hang back as many paces as you dare, and give me a nightingale whistle if you need me." He headed down to the riverbank and snuck along the bushes, knife at the ready.

Sere considered tossing some shotgun pellets into the river in order to call in some aquatic help, but Bart was moving with the swiftness of his SEAL training. *We have the upper hand, but only so long as we stay ahead. I don't even know what a school of catfish could do for us.*

Bart moved with the rhythms of the swamp: stepping in time to the crickets to mask the sound of his footsteps, dancing between the brush and the river with the changing shadows, and hunkering down as silent and invisible as a black cat at the slightest unexpected sound. Even with Sere's training and knowledge of the swamp, she found it hard to keep up. When he darted into the trees, she lost him.

Damn it. She wanted to whistle for him, but whatever danger had caused him to slip in among the brush would also likely prevent him from answering. Instead, she nestled against the folds of a cypress trunk and tried to blend in with the roots. The vantage point wasn't the best, but there were only so many places he could have gone. She relied on the tree's protection while focusing beyond Bart's potential location to what had attracted his attention. Without worrying about keeping up, she was free to devote all of her awareness to the section of wetland. *There's an alligator sleeping in the tall grass, an owl keeping lookout overhead, and a family of nutrias feeding in the brush. None of them seem disturbed. What the hell did you see, Bart? And where the fuck are you?*

The alligator adjusted his position, no doubt attracted by the grazing river rats. Instead of scampering toward the brush, however, it lunged upright. *Bart!* The Navy SEAL slashed backhanded at a tree trunk with his all-black combat knife. He struck with such force that Sere thought he was trying to chop it down in one swoop, but instead of the light-tan color of freshly exposed wood, dark-red blood oozed from under his blade.

"You can come out now, Sere," Bart said while keeping the knife firmly in place.

"How the hell did you know where I was—or where *he* was?"

"Years of training and even more years of covert actions."

She approached the tree to see the result of Bart's mission. The knife impaled the demon through the neck and into the tree behind him. The location of the blow had missed his vocal cords.

"Why didn't you cut off his head?" she asked.

"I thought you might have some questions for their leader. Based on his skills at evasion, this puppet isn't your average doppelgänger. This is also the demon that led my abduction."

She tried to see the squad from Bart's perspective. The guard at the cabin had been there merely to assist the inquisitor. From his lack of skills, that had to be the lowliest position of the group. As for her interrogator, even he admitted he was little more than a lab flunky. The attack force Joe was dealing with had to be made up of nothing more than foot shoulders. A leader wouldn't be so easily distracted as to chase after a lone commando.

She walked up to the snarling demon. "Who are you working for?"

"Like I'm going to tell you. Cut off my head and get it over with."

"Not the worst idea." Bart twisted the blade.

From the hatred in the demon's eyes, Sere could tell he wasn't going to talk simply because of threats. "You're not afraid of being decapitated?"

"Why should I be?" the demon demanded in defiance. "I'll simply be regenerated in hell. You're losing, little girl."

Deep down, she feared he was right. Each time a gang made its escape, the doppelgängers learned something new. "Maybe, but you'll be nothing more than a mindless drone."

"Not me."

His two words sent a shiver to her bones. She had heard that arrogant self-confidence before. Even in his contorted expression of anger, she made out the high cheekbones, aristocratic forehead, and deep-set beady eyes of their once-shared heritage.

"Kill him. I've seen what I need to." She leaned in to the demon's ear before Bart completed the cut. "I may not know exactly who you are, but I've got a pretty good idea of where to look. And I guarantee you will not be coming back even if I have to kill your real myself."

Only a red glow remained in the demon's eyes after Bart swung his knife to the side like a paper cutter. Once the body had slumped to the ground, the Navy SEAL allowed the head to roll off his blade. "Mind explaining that last interaction?"

"Later," Sere said. "We've got to find Joe, finish off these doppelfuckers, and get our tails back to New Orleans as fast as possible."

SERE NEARLY TRIPPED over Joe's Honda Blackbird covered in leaves. "Found it."

Without the threat of a demon rear guard, she and Bart had quickly made their way back along the highway to the stashed motorcycle.

Bart knelt down and grabbed the handlebars. "Give me a hand getting this thing out of the muck. We need to roll it to some solid ground before firing it up."

She turned around and put her butt to the seat so she could push it up with her legs. "For a lightweight bike, this thing is a handful."

Once it was upright, Bart admired its lines. He let out a low whistle. "She is pretty. Must be killer fast too."

"You have no idea." Sere got behind the rear tire so she could push as Bart pulled on the handlebars. In less than a hundred feet, they had both tires clear of the waterlogged soil. "Want to take the controls?"

He looked at her out of the corners of his eyes. "Second time in one day that you're letting me take the lead. That must be some kind of record."

"I'm still a little woozy from the demon's experiment, and this thing requires complete attention. Just don't gun it and drop me off the back."

He swung his leg over the seat and hit the starter. "Purrs like a kitten. I'm guessing Joe made a few refinements."

"Yeah, and he's going to be pissed that I totaled the machine he built for me." She climbed on after Bart and wrapped her arms around his abs. The memory of seeing him naked—and fucking Edie—made Sere glad her body didn't betray any outward signals of her lust.

Though meant for road use, Bart scooted the Honda through the leaves and twigs and back onto the highway like he was playing with a dirt bike. Once he stopped power sliding it through the mud, he lined it up on the asphalt and laid into the throttle as if he'd owned the bike all his life. He hadn't.

Sere hung on for dear life as the Blackbird tried living up to its name by lifting the front tire three feet off the ground. "Would you mind *not* killing us both?"

"Aren't you the one who likes making a grand entrance? Just hang on while I get the feel of this thing."

Usually Sere resented the need for a helmet, but for the first time, she kind of missed the technologically paranormal head protection Joe had worked up. It was probably buried in the swamp's silt by now, being played with by catfish.

Bart put the front tire back on the road just before

carving into the first curve. Trying to distract herself from the blur of asphalt that threatened to reach up and graze her knee, Sere focused on the differences between Joe's bike and the one she'd crashed. Heavier and meaner, this one didn't seem to care about the will of the rider—though the impression could have easily been due to Bart being at the controls. When he straightened the bike out of the curve, it again shot forward like a bullet out of a gun. Even in third gear, the rear wheel squealed against the road. The front tire lifted again but in a way that felt like a more controlled liftoff.

Bart practically threw the motorcycle into the next curve. "This thing is crazy fun," he yelled.

She lifted her head from between his shoulder blades and put her mouth to his ear. "We're here to fight demons, not get your rocks off. Pay attention. That next curve is where I lost it, and there's no way of knowing if the booby trap could claim this bike as well."

He slammed on the brakes and twisted the bike perpendicular to the road. They skidded to a stop just before the bend. From over the side of the road, the smell of burnt oil, rubber, and wood wafted through the air.

The moment the bike came to rest, Sere hopped off the back, ran to the edge of the road, and yanked out her shotgun. "Come and get me, you doppelfuckers!" She cocked the gun and let a round fly over the trees. If Lefty was within range, he would heed her call.

A return shotgun blast sounded from across the river. "The demon is coming at you from your left," Joe yelled. "Be careful. He's wearing your helmet."

Shit. With the readouts, the demon would have a clear view of her. She cocked the shotgun and stared through the telescopic sight at the river's edge, but nothing moved.

Bart snuck up beside her. "I'm going to head down the road a hundred yards to see if I can spot him," he whispered.

"Don't go any farther than that, and listen for my whistle. And whatever you do, don't die."

"I'll do my best." He kissed her on the cheek so casually she wondered if it had been an automatic response or something more.

She hurried off the road and climbed the first large oak tree that overhung the river. The demon might have any one of a number of weapons. The bikers who frequented Bart's establishment seldom carried their arsenals into the bar, but that didn't mean they didn't have guns and knives stashed in the saddlebags of their Harleys. Anything left on the bikes would have been inventoried for use by the lead demon. The doppelgänger Bart had sliced up was no dummy.

She lay out flat on a moss-covered limb and aimed her shotgun at the river's edge. Though she still couldn't make out so much as a single blade of grass moving, she knew Joe would be working his way along the shoreline, searching for his prey. *Come on, Joe. We've got work to do.*

But as one minute stretched to two and then ten, Sere worried they were being outfoxed by the demon. She rolled to her side and looked down along the river. Bart had to be fairly close by. If he were far off, she'd have felt his absence. She whistled a nightingale song.

A light breeze preceded his arrival at the base of her tree

as if he'd been nothing more than a leaf blown to her. "This is taking too long," he whispered up to her.

"I agree. What should we do?"

Bart searched the river. "We need to get across."

"Why?" With Joe on the other side, having the demon trapped between them made sense. Joining forces would only leave their enemy room to maneuver. A cold chill ran down her back.

"I'm concerned about Joe. He had to face six demons alone, and now he's being awfully quiet over there. I'd expected a signal of some type to indicate he was okay. Have you picked up anything from him?"

Sere sprang down from the tree and rushed toward the river without worrying about being seen or heard by the demon. Bart was right. Joe should have whistled. During practice stakeouts, he always comforted her with his range of wildlife interpretations.

She dove into the water without a thought to her clothing or the dangers that lurked around her. A splash behind her let her know Bart wasn't wasting time being secretive either. *When I get out of this river, either Joe will be standing on the water's edge, angry at me for giving away our location, or there will be no sign of him, and Bart's concerns will be confirmed.*

She dug in hard against the current, pumping her arms and legs with everything she had. When her fingers hit sand, she popped up to her feet and ran toward the tree line. The hope of finding Joe there to greet her seemed like the delusion of a little girl whose father had gone to war but who nonetheless expected to see him when she got home from school.

"Joe!" she yelled into the forest.

Bart rushed up beside her and motioned for her to be still. "Stay quiet for a moment and listen."

She did her best, but the adrenaline rushing through her body made it hard to be calm enough to detect much of anything.

Bart prowled forward like a bloodhound that had just picked up a scent. She kept close behind him as he pushed aside the tree branches and worked into the shadowy forest.

"Down here." Joe's voice sounded like it came from under Sere's feet.

She dropped to her knees and started pulling the leaf canopy off of him. The entire improvised tent was soaking wet. "You couldn't have found any dry vegetation?"

"It was dry when I pulled it over me." His voice was much too weak.

She touched her hand to her nose and smelled the metallic odor of blood. Bart put his hand on her shoulder and pulled her back. "Let me have a look."

She caught the relief on Joe's face that Bart was the one doing the investigating. Bart carefully lifted a branch covered in moss then set it back over Joe's body. "What can I do?"

Joe took his hand out of the muck and put it on Bart's. "Give her your assessment, then let me have a minute alone with her."

Bart put the man's hand over the camouflage covering then motioned to Sere to join him away from Joe. "He's dying. There's a bullet wound in his gut and another in his chest. From the amount of blood soaking the vegetation around him, I'd guess he's down to his last few minutes. That man is a bull. I don't know anyone who could have survived this long with those wounds. He's only hanging on to say goodbye."

Tears filled Sere's eyes, making it impossible to see. She fell to her knees and crawled back to her mentor, father figure, and friend. "What happened?"

He pointed at his cracked motorcycle helmet beside the tree. "The demon had the drop on me. With the other helmet, the monster was able to see what I was up to and read my vitals from the shared connection. While I hunted down the other six doppelgängers, this one set the trap. It was a good fight. I decapitated four demons and injured the other two enough to ensure that the alligators had two good meals. I watched all six demons meet their end. When I heard the motorcycle fire up, I got too excited. It's been a long time since I was on the hunt, and my relief that you were okay got the better of me. I worked my way to the river without anticipating a trap. If it hadn't been for you pulling your warrior-goddess routine on the road, my adversary would have decapitated me the way I'd done the others."

Sere wanted to fight, argue, demand that he hang on—anything but sit quietly and watch him die. But Joe would be the first to tell her that comrades in arms accepted their fates—and worse, the fates of those closest to them. She put her hand on his chest. Blood covered it, making it feel like the marshy ground. "Anything I think to say sounds trite."

He put his hand over hers. "I'm proud of you and always have been. It has been an honor and a privilege to help train the world's savior."

"No final snarky rejoinder?" She sniffled back her tears.

"Not this time, Serephine. Love is understood more than spoken. Neither of us needs the words. There's a black leather satchel under the floorboards in the bedroom of my cabin." His words were lost to a fit of coughing that forced him to turn on his side. When he stopped, she knew he was gone.

9

---

*S*ere let Bart lead her back to the road. The loas of the dead would be hovering around at any minute to escort Joseph Cazenave to the nirvana he so richly deserved. At least, that was Sere's take, and if the loas had the audacity to think otherwise, they'd have her to deal with. Though a demon had done the deed, the monster hadn't hung around for Joe's passing. His soul didn't belong to them. The logical argument gave her some comfort, but until she got eyes inside hell to know what was really going on, she'd never be sure. If the worst case was that Joe was in hell, at least the other innocent souls the demons had captured would have a warrior on their side.

She sat on the pavement, looking out at the swamp. The heavy feeling of having just lost her most trusted ally and the rock that had sustained her since the moment she'd been tossed in hell made it impossible to move.

Bart rounded up Joe's helmet, knives, and rifle. The

growing pile of belongings sat next to Sere like a fellow mourner. It reminded her of Larry's mechanic tools. The things were worse than useless without the people who knew how to use them—a mockery of what they had been. Just like her.

Bart sat next to her opposite Joe's belongings and stared out over the swamp. "So how do we get that pellet out of you?"

It was a fair question. The pellet was holding them back. Riding the motorcycles to their next disaster would be a problem if she couldn't be more than a hundred feet away from Bart.

"Knowing Joe, there will be a med kit somewhere on his motorcycle."

Bart turned to her. His worried look didn't inspire confidence in his ability to do what needed to be done. "I thought you said if the demon scientist hooked you up, the pellet would be pulled through your body."

"It will." There wasn't much point in hiding the truth. "The demon intended on slashing me then wrapping the bandage around the wound. That meant while I was hooked to Jennifer, the pellet would be racing around inside me like a ricocheting bullet and not take the most direct path out of my body. I have no idea what would happen with me being damaged while trying to heal. We need to use the bandage more like an electromagnet to pull the pellet out in one direction."

He got up and opened the Blackbird's front cowlings. Joe liked to travel light. With all of his weapons already on the highway, only the small black bag was left nestled in the bottom of the tight compartment.

"Got it." Bart opened the bag. "Looks like he had a lot of faith in your skills. There's only one small bandage in here with the cord and cell phone." He handed her the rolled-up wire-laced cloth. "How do you want to do this?"

She unzipped her leather riding pants and pressed the roll to her abdomen. The feeling of wanting to vomit from one specific point in her gut was like having swallowed an angry yellow jacket. "Unspool the cord and take the cell phone to the bend in the road. You'll need to stay with it until I tell you to end the connection. No matter how much pain I'm in, you have to stay with the phone. Understand?"

He handed her the end of the cable. "I've seen you in pain. You're like a wildcat hissing and scratching at everyone dumb enough to offer help. Once was enough. Don't worry. I'll keep my distance."

She favored him with a smile. She knew his show of wounded pride was just a cover for not wanting to see her suffer. "Damn straight. Since this isn't a normal object, I'm not sure what the effects will be. If I lose consciousness once it's out, unroll the bandage, wrap it around my torso, and use the Velcro strip at the end to hold it together. Then go back to the phone and hit the app again. I'm going to need Jennifer's strength to repair the damage. With the bandage around me, the professor's equipment will shut down once I'm whole again."

Bart unwound the cord and walked a safe distance away. In an overly dramatic way, he held the phone in one hand and aimed a finger with the other. "Ready?"

"Don't make me laugh, asshole."

"I'll take that as a yes." He punched the screen.

The searing pain of the yellow-jacket stone coming to life and chewing its way out of her gut had her screaming. Though only an inch of flesh separated the shotgun pellet from the bandage, the dissolving body matter wasn't a pain any human would understand. She pressed the bandage harder into her flexed abdomen, willing the pellet to move faster. The red haze of her demon side struck so hard she wondered if the blood from her wound had squirted over her eyes. Her scream of pain became a dark howl of rage.

Once the pellet from hell broke the surface of her skin, her arm, the bandage, and the blood-soaked paranormal stone fell to her side. She barely got the word "done" out before everything faded to black.

Jennifer pulled out of her husband's arms and twisted around on the couch. "I'll be right back."

From the deep breath he took when she moved and his half-closed eyes, she could tell that Henry had been more asleep than awake. "Do you want me to pause the movie?"

She kissed him on the cheek before getting up. "Don't bother. I'll only be a minute."

Sere felt as groggy as a little kid who'd just been picked up to be taken to bed. She watched through Jennifer's eyes as the woman looked around the kitchen. "I've got wine or coffee," Jennifer said. "I know you'd prefer whiskey, but that would involve coming up with a cover story for Henry as the wet bar is next to the television. It's only fair to warn you, I'm not much good at hiding things from him."

"Coffee," Sere said. "And maybe a cookie if you have any left."

From behind the woman's face, Sere found it remarkable how many muscles were used to create the wife and mother's knowing smile. "So that's the temptation you can't resist. I'll remember that. It'll be our little secret." Jennifer took an oversized cookie and the bowl-shaped cup filled with steaming coffee out to the back porch. "So I imagine there's some life-or-death battle are you are currently in the middle of dealing with. I hope you're not lying mortally wounded beside some river." She took a bite of the cookie as casually as if they were discussing changing channels.

"Joe was stabbed to death by one of the demons."

The bite of cookie lodged halfway down Jennifer's throat. She set the remainder on her dress. Tears filled her eyes. *I'm sorry.* The emotion was so pervasive that words would never have conveyed it.

"You didn't even know him." Sere didn't mean to be crass, but her connection to her mentor wasn't something the homemaker would understand.

"Don't be cruel," Jennifer said. "He saved my life. When you prompted our fight with him, I learned a lot about myself—both the good part of my caring and the bad part of holding on too tightly. I'd guess that was just a taste of what your life has been like with him as your teacher."

"He was more than that." Sere could cover her emotions with snarkiness or bravado while in her body, but as pure spirit, she had no place to hide what she truly felt. "Most of who I am, I owe to Joe. He was the only one who treated me like I wasn't some fragile porcelain doll while I was growing up. Even when I was a little girl, he treated me as an equal."

Jennifer blew on the hot coffee and took a sip to finally help the cookie down. "I envy you."

Though she knew Jennifer wished she were stronger, more adventurous, and braver, Sere felt those weren't the attributes the homemaker was referring to. "For the love of God, why?"

"You hang onto the people you love."

Sere had never experienced the hidden truth that Jennifer reached with her simple comment. "I've seen you with Bobby and Henry," she countered.

"That's not the same." Jennifer stared at the night sky as if searching for an answer to Sere's confusion. "My father is still alive, but I hardly ever talk to him. It's not that we don't get along. We just grew apart. Most of the people I've known have drifted out of my life. You don't just fight evil—you fight to keep those you care about. That's what I envy."

"Fat lot of good it does me when they die anyway. Joe would still be alive if he hadn't tried to rescue me. All the people I'm close to have risked their necks for me—even you. And Joe isn't the first to lose his life in the quest to save me." The memory of how Larry and Kelly had been so kind to Sere—a stranger who staggered into the diner covered in oil—and had been the first to lose their lives to a demon was something that would haunt her forever.

Jennifer ate more of the cookie as if offering Sere comfort in the form of chocolate chips. "Now you're sounding like me."

Jennifer was right. Sere needed to snap out of it. Joe would have been the first to smack her for her self-pity.

"I suppose I'm still figuring out how to rely on others. Protecting those closest to me is easier than letting them put it all on the line for me."

"Life isn't supposed to be bland," Jennifer said. "The adventures that truly bond people together are never easy."

Sere had to say something to keep the homemaker from following her lead. "I do what I have to do. I didn't choose this life. You make it sound like a camping trip or something. I'm trying to prevent hell from taking over this world."

"Exactly. Who wouldn't want to join you in that quest? Mourn Joe. He was a good man, and you lost someone important. But don't for a minute think he would have wanted any less than what you gave him: a true and noble life quest."

Her debate with Jennifer confirmed that the connection was returning Sere to full strength. "Maybe you're right. Lord knows Joe would have made the same argument. Sometimes it seemed like he'd spent his life preparing for my problems."

Jennifer got up and brushed the cookie crumbs from her dress. "You're starting to fade, and I need to get back to Henry. He never sleeps well if I'm not next to him, even if we are just watching some cheesy movie. I hope you're feeling better, my sweet badass demon-hunting heroine."

1 O

*S*ere came back to her body hunched over and holding her stomach. "That was a bad one."

Bart was still rolling up the bandage. "Think you can ride? We need to get after that last demon. Since he didn't head back here for a motorcycle, he must have slipped away in the river. He can't be far."

Sere was grateful that Bart didn't want to discuss her connection to Jennifer, or worse, Joe's death. "Fuck that doppelhole." Sere felt the icy-cold tentacles of anger tighten around her heart. "So long as that chickenshit isn't going to come after us, we've got a bigger problem. I recognized the lead demon. He had high cheekbones, deep-set penetrating eyes, tall aristocratic forehead, and sharply angled jaw. Sound like anyone you know?"

"You could be talking about half of the city," Bart said.

Sere was grateful her doppelgänger body was the result

of a different ancestry than her soul. She'd never be recognized as a member of the powerful elite. "My father, Baron Malveaux, had similar features to that demon. Each time that living devil forced a new upper-class New Orleans woman into sexual indentured servitude, he took her as his own concubine before abandoning her to his brothels. That ensured that each rich, respectable family carried at least one of his heirs. Within the first two generations after his death, the Laroque branch of the family tree realized the importance of nurturing those genetic markers."

Bart stuffed the cell phone, cord, and bandage in the black medical bag. "Hang on a minute. As his daughter, you died before any of these family shenanigans started. How would you know what the Laroque family was up to?"

Sere remembered Kendell's lectures on their shared heritage. The poor woman had tried so hard to explain why the baron's history mattered, but as a child, Sere couldn't have given a rat's ass. Now she was glad Kendell had spent so much time drilling the information into her head.

"Kendell knew it would be important for me to learn about our family history. I can see now how right she was. Many in New Orleans consider bank president Marjory Laroque and her brother—former Chief of Police Gerald Laroque—to be the culmination of the family's aspirations. Those people are mistaken. For a time, Marjory's son, Lincoln Laroque, held the real power in the city. When my father decided to retake what he thought was his rightful place among the living, he wanted to use the most powerful man in New Orleans—and also the one who most closely resembled him in aspiration and appearance. That demon leader you decapitated wasn't Lincoln's doppelgänger, but he must have been from a close relative. And there are three unaccounted-for demons headed toward New Orleans right now. I'm willing to bet my gator-skin boots there's another Laroque doppelgänger leading the charge."

"So what?" Bart asked. "Since every doppelgänger has a real in New Orleans, it would only make sense that eventually a member of the Laroque family would surface in the swamp. It's not like the death-and-demon replacement of a member of the most powerful family in New Orleans is going to go unnoticed."

Sere looked up at Bart, envious of his ability to stand and function. "The demon said even if I killed him, he'd regenerate in hell without being wiped clean like any other doppelgänger. That means someone already understands some of the professor's technology."

Bart shrugged. "Powerful family in life. Powerful family in death. Not much new about that. I'm still not seeing the new danger."

They didn't have all day, but she needed to explain the situation to him. He had a right to know what he was up against if he was going to join her on her next mission. "That's just one piece of the puzzle. I suspected I had an enemy in hell. During that demonic experiment, Sanguine told me the real danger is coming from someone in this reality, not hers."

"Someone in life is calling forth the demons? Why?"

"I asked the same thing." Sere looked into Bart's soulful eyes. "It's because of me. Sanguine didn't want to spell it out for fear someone might be listening, but I think she figured out what our enemy is up to. I'm a human soul living in an immortal body. That's the kind of thing some people might find enticing. People with money and influence, like the Laroques, would consider immortality their ultimate prize even if they did become part demon to obtain it. Researching how my father traveled between dimensions and created me would be just a matter of finding his journals. That would have been the hard part. Based on this demon outbreak, they must be ready to run some tests, which means they have read at least some of his writings." She spread her arms out to display her body. "They already have the first successful experiment in front of them. I'm proof that the two parts can coexist in the same doppelgänger body. And the professor has made it clear that he has enough data to keep me going even after Jennifer has died. The same would be true for any of the professor's projections that escape hell. The next step for our demon scientist would be to try to reproduce the results."

Bart stroked the stubble on his chin. "Let's take this one step at a time. Even if the Laroque doppelgängers could regenerate and retain what they knew after decapitation, the family wouldn't risk one of their powerful elite—not for the first test anyway. But they'd also not want a bunch of random immortal test subjects running around New Orleans. Which means the three-demon breakaway contingent isn't going to waste time on a joy-ride killing spree."

Sere expected that the three-demon force was headed to some Laroque stronghold. She assumed Bart's military training was leading him to the same conclusion. "What are you thinking?"

"We have one guinea-pig doppelgänger with two guards who might not be there strictly for that demon's protection. If I were told I was being taken somewhere to subjugate my identity to another, I might not go willingly. Even if the real and the doppelgänger are mostly the same person, there's a hell of a difference between being the one taking over versus the one being potentially extinguished."

"Good point." For the first time since she'd watched Joe's life fade away, she felt something resembling a sense of mission. "If the three aren't working in unison, that would slow them down and buy us a little time. But why wouldn't the Laroque family just send an armored truck to pick him up? Seems risky leaving the transfer to a couple of demons with desires of their own."

"Your friend Fisher has proven money can't be spent without leaving a trail. The Laroque elite wouldn't risk their involvement in the potential demon apocalypse being discovered. Too many people might be watching. They won't tip their hand until they've created their immortal. Remember, this is just their first attempt."

"So they're relying on the demons bringing the doppeldummy to New Orleans," Sere said as she worked her body off the pavement, "but they couldn't just bring him to the real's house. We're talking about transferring a soul. That's, like, deep voodoo shit. I can kill a doppelgänger and under the right circumstances have that energy transfer to its real, but that's because the demonic energy is amped up in hell. It's like grounding an electrical charge. Transferring a soul *into* a demon would take some work."

"So the immediate questions are where are they taking him, and who would have those kinds of skills?"

"Once Kendell and Myles secured my father in hell, they put the voodoo community under tight control. Even with all of the Laroque family's power and money, no practitioner is going to cross the city's paranormal-power couple. That means our demons won't be headed for any of the secret voodoo parlors."

Bart leaned against the seat of the Blackbird motorcycle. "The Laroques wouldn't let someone as powerful as a potential immortal out of their grasp. They'd have to base their experiments somewhere in New Orleans where no one would see what was happening. What's the most secure and secret spot you can think of that they might use?"

Gerald Laroque hadn't been in charge of the force in more than a decade. That removed an interrogation room in police headquarters from Sere's consideration. But Sere had one other idea.

"One of the bank vaults in New Orleans Bank and Trust. It would make perfect sense. Marjory now runs the bank that my evil father made the seat of his power." Sere shivered at the memory of being locked in the baron's magical iron room. "This is all starting to hit a little close to home for me. We need to get word to Fisher to look out for the three demons and let him know where they might be going. Head down the road until you get a signal, and I'll round up our gear."

Bart pulled out his phone, but instead of powering it up, he turned it over and yanked out the battery.

"What the hell are you doing?" she asked.

"You remember a little while ago you asked what I knew about GPS technology?"

"Yeah. You said it was none of my business."

Bart shook his head and snickered. "That's not what I said. My training is classified." He threw the pieces onto the blacktop and stomped on the brittle plastic, shattering it to bits. "My personal phone could have been easily hacked. Even if I had a burner phone, it wouldn't be that hard for them to use it to tap into Fisher's computers, phones, cars—you name it. As the former chief of police, Gerald Laroque would still have access to every phone call in the greater New Orleans area as well as GPS locators. If we call Fisher, we will just be painting a bull's-eye on his back."

"Do you still have your wallet?" Sere asked.

Bart looked confused and patted the bulge in the back of his pants. "Those demons make lousy robbers. Once the leader took the credit card out of my wallet to pay for gassing up the bikes, he tossed the billfold on the ground. I wasn't about to just leave it there."

"Fisher figured out where to send me based on the demons' use of your credit card."

"I think I see where you're going." Bart pulled out the worn leather wallet and checked the contents. "Fortunately, I do carry more than one card. If I put nine dollars and eleven cents' worth of gas on my business card, that should at least tip Fisher off that there's a problem and who to contact. Then all I need to do is stop by the bar and let Edie know what to tell Fisher. Do you think he'll know to stay off his phones?"

"He's pretty damn smart," Sere said. The possibility of seeing Bart with Edie after witnessing their fuck session left Sere concerned that a bar brawl might be in her future, but even so, she couldn't let the woman be emotionally blindsided. "When you tell Edie about Joe, realize she kind of had a crush on him."

TALKING out the future mission was wildly different than getting on with her life. Sere stood next to the Honda Blackbird as if it were a spectral transport to the afterlife. "What am I supposed to do with you? I've never felt so lost."

Bart wrapped his arm around her waist. "Joe would have wanted you to have it. Just focus on one action at a time. I'll take the lead. We'll get some gas in order to notify Fisher, then we'll stop off at the bar."

At least he didn't give her some bullshit about one day everything being okay again. She secured Joe's shotgun, knives, and personal effects in the small storage of the cowling. The helmet that had given her such a forceful connection to Joe lay at her feet.

"What about that?"

"It might come in handy. I'll throw it on the back of my bike. We don't dare power it up, however, in case the remaining demon is wearing its match."

She fired up the menacing motorcycle like a dragon she intended to ride into battle. "I need to fight someone."

He looked her over. "Maybe it'd be best if I go to the bar alone. Once we fill up, you can head down to Joe's cabin, and I'll meet you there. I don't need you giving my already shorthanded staff more work by creating havoc." He walked down the highway to the group of stolen bikes tossed haphazardly into a field.

Asshole. But he's probably right. She revved the Blackbird's engine while waiting for him. Unfortunately, with the exhaust dampener, the bike sounded like a bunny trying to puff itself up rather than a high-performance beast threatening to chase down everyone within earshot.

As Bart finally rode up next to her, she shouted over the Ducati's engine noise, "Lay into your ride. This thing doesn't know how to go slow." She flipped on the light switch, feeling like she was violating Joe's modifications to the bike. *And now everyone can see me.*

Once Bart was well past her, she twisted the throttle and lifted her feet from the ground. Without the beefy Navy SEAL's added weight, the motorcycle shot through the first curve like a racehorse without a rider. The wind tousled Sere's short hair. For just a moment, she felt as if Joe's spirit was ruffling her locks and teasing her to go faster. Bart was a couple of hundred yards ahead.

I need to see what you can do. She hammered the gearshift and blasted the bike down the road. Without the technological advantage of the helmet, her understanding of the road ahead and its obstacles was limited to what she could see.

Don't get careless. The thought could have easily been a residual warning from Joe. "I have no intentions of crashing another bike, old man. But you'd be the first to tell me I need to understand my limits if I have any hope of surpassing them. Don't worry. I'm beginning to understand the effects my recklessness has on others."

When she rounded the next curve, Bart was right in front of her. The glowing-green speedometer on the Blackbird read eighty miles per hour. "Sorry, my friend, but you're going to have to catch me." Sere steered the Blackbird around Bart's Monster and tore into the open road. She snugged down tight against the gas tank. The small windscreen barely provided enough protection for her to see what lay ahead. Her eyes watered from the air and emotion, but being back on the speed demon made her feel alive.

A bike horn sounded from far behind her. "Shit, we were supposed to stop for gas." She hit the brakes and swung the bike around, skidding the rear tire. The motorcycle accelerated in the opposite direction through the black smoke of burned rubber she'd just created a minute earlier. The cloud of eye-watering smoke caused her to lose sight of Bart.

The tire skid made it obvious which exit he had taken. She pulled into the brightly lit service station at the base of the exit just as Bart was taking off his helmet. "Sorry. I got a little carried away."

"I noticed." He lifted the gas nozzle then plugged it into his tank. Slowly pulling the lever, he dispensed an exact $9.11 into the tank. "How's yours set for fuel?"

As with eating, Sere seldom paid much attention to the necessities of motorcycle riding. "I guess I should fill up."

He looked over her shoulder. "You're down to the reserve. Yeah, you should fill up." He handed her the credit card. "Maybe Fisher will get the hint that there's two of us."

The lump that had sat at the base of Sere's throat moved down to her stomach. "And only the two of us."

11

S ere sat on the motionless Blackbird in front of Joe's cabin. As if conducting some philosophical experiment, she held onto the idea that as long as she didn't enter the dwelling, he might still be inside. She remained planted on the vinyl seat, wishing illogically that it were so.

"This is crazy. I've got work to do, and I'm being emotional." Even as a child in hell, she'd had better control of her reactions. "Must be that damned blood in my veins."

She swung her leg off the motorcycle. At least Joe didn't set booby traps in his home, just in his hidden caches. Her last visit to the cabin, however, had resulted in her being attacked by a demon lying in wait. And there was another demon out there somewhere—one that had already proven its expertise against one of the most skilled professionals Sere knew.

She drew the shotgun from the cowling and made sure it was fully loaded. "I hope to hell you are here. I could use the fight, and I'd be happy to be rid of you before facing your cohorts."

Instead of heading to the front door, she snuck around the side of the cabin. Since the demons had taken the technological bandage from Joe's hidden cache, they might have absconded with his high-speed swamp boat as well. She couldn't afford to take any more chances with people's safety—neither with those she cared about nor with herself. Putting herself in danger had a way of making those closest to her make dumb-shit moves to save her.

The field of pine needles had been raked smooth. There were enough randomly strewn newly fallen needles, however, to prove that Joe had been the one setting his security system and not some demon recently trying to trick her. She cocked the shotgun and crept under the deck. The small dock just offshore rocked from the gentle lapping of the water, but there was no boat moored to it. Not that it mattered. With all of the hidden bends and beaches along the river the demon could have stashed the boat within a hundred yards and Sere wouldn't see it. She couldn't shake the feeling that she wasn't alone, even though every indication argued against the hairs that stuck up on the back of her neck.

"So this is what you're going to leave me with, Joe? That sixth sense, eyes-in-the-back-of-my-head nervous feeling you kept saying was something that couldn't be taught?" Sere wasn't sure she liked it.

She ran a tactical assessment to figure out where her adversary might be hiding. Anyone who was out there would have seen her pull up. Her hell-based lab-geek abductor had made it clear they couldn't kill her. They needed her to be alive but not necessarily walking around freely killing every demon she met. If they did capture her, they'd be free to run whatever experiments they could imagine.

Her mind was slowly clearing from the overwhelming emotion of loss. Heading into the cabin would have been foolish. Even if there was no one hiding in the shadows, the breakaway contingent had likely set some surprise for her on their way to New Orleans.

"Is that why you hightailed it after killing Joe?" she asked quietly to whatever boogey demon might be hiding in the shadows. "Did your compatriots expect you to come here and find me dangling by my boots?" She didn't really care if the demon heard her. He had her helmet. Though she hadn't played with all of its little gadgets, it probably had enhanced hearing to go along with the night vision. "I have to accept that you can see and hear me," she said as much to herself as to the demon. "But you don't want to come out to play? Maybe you think I'll grow bored and step into your trap. You are kind of a doppelshit. You know that? I'll bet you pulled the same game on Joe."

A water moccasin swam along the top of the river and slithered onto shore.

"Hello, my friend. Now, what would make you leave the comfort of your den at this hour? You look a little too well-fed to be out hunting." She quickly snuck into a bramble between the far side of the cabin and the river. The dock continued to bob quietly, leaving a small trail of disturbed water as it remained anchored against the flow. The marsh grass that hung onto the beat-up Styrofoam floats waved with the current. A clump let go and drifted downstream.

"So that's where you are, you clever little demon." Sere wanted to abandon the gun, pull out her knife, and dive in for a good fight, but that would constitute reckless action. "You can't stay under there forever." Like her, the doppelgänger needed to breathe. And though Joe's helmets were impressive, she doubted they were designed for use underwater.

The water moccasin undulated up the small incline to Sere's feet and lifted its head toward her shotgun. "Not a bad idea. Where there's one of you, there's often a whole nest." She ejected one of the shotgun shells, crushed the plastic casing, and heaved the pellets over the dock. "I wonder if there's something more dramatic out there." Popping another shell out of the gun, she skipped it over the water. It submerged halfway across the river.

Ripples disturbed the surface, indicating that the aquatic animals had heeded her call. She ran along the riverbank and jumped onto the dock before the demon had a chance to figure out her attack. "Run or fight. Either way, I'll be ready for you." She aimed the shotgun around the water at every sign of movement.

The dock rocked so hard to the side that Sere lost her footing and pulled the trigger, sending shotgun pellets into the brush. She grabbed the cleat to avoid tumbling into the water but lost her gun over the side. *So you want to play dirty? Fine by me.* She pulled hard at the brass fitting to get her feet under her. In one catlike launch, she was crouched upright with her knife in hand ready for whatever presented itself.

The demon swung up from the edge of the dock. Instead of attacking, however, it pulled the motorcycle helmet off. Long tangled strands of black hair fell over the doppelgirl's shoulders. "Don't kill me."

She raised her hands, but from the bent shoulders and elbows, Sere could tell the stance wasn't completely submissive. The plea of leniency could easily transition to a claws-out attack.

Sere bent low. Her knife gleamed in the moonlight. "You killed my friend. You don't belong here. I have no reason to show you mercy. You don't get to live."

The girl kept her arms wide. "You above all people know existence is cheap in hell. I'd say I was sorry about your friend, but sorrow and friendship are two human experiences I couldn't possibly understand."

Sere gripped the knife handle so hard her forearm ached. *Joe's knife. What could be more fitting than slicing that doppelwhore's throat with his Ranger blade?* "You're nothing more than a demon from hell. And now I'm sending you back." She dove at the demon, expecting some form of countermove.

The doppelbitch rolled to her side like a gymnast and narrowly escaped Sere's slashing attack. She came back up to the same hands-wide stance she'd started with. "I don't want to go back there. The harvesters are running the place. Just look at my face."

Sere struggled to keep her demonic side in check. Every

instinct, human and otherwise, argued for a swift decapitation of the conniving demon. "You killed Joe."

The demon pulled her swamp-plastered hair from her face. "Will you please just fucking *look?*"

Gritting her teeth, Sere gazed at the demon, tracing the youthful, round, feminine face. "You're the waif I saw in hell during my dream. So what?" The night in hell's version of the French Quarter, fighting a harvester, was only one of many nightmares Sere would just as soon forget.

"I helped you escape."

There was nothing worse than a demon who would change a story for her own benefit. "You did not help me escape. You didn't do a damn thing except tell me help was on the way. I could have figured that out on my own when Lefty woke me up. You just watched me do battle then used Sanguine's name to manipulate me."

"You want the truth? Fine. You seemed like someone worth knowing. I'd never seen anyone outfight a harvester. But I wasn't lying about the goddess. Sanguine took care of those who lived in hell's gutters before she was abducted. Without her, I had nothing to lose in trying to escape."

Sere began to see the connection. "Kendell watches over the homeless in life, and Sanguine must have done the same for the matching doppelgängers in hell. That still doesn't earn you a place among the living."

"I can help you."

"Like you did out in the swamp?" The knife in Sere's hand seemed to be begging to be put to use against the demon waif's throat. "You killed my friend then ran like a little chickenshit demon."

"Had I stayed, you'd have killed me, and your friend would have ended up in the hell you're trying to send me back to."

Sere turned the knife as she thought, *So those souls are in hell*. "Start talking. If I don't like what I hear, you'll lose your head before you finish the sentence."

"Other than your friend, has my contingent killed any humans?"

Beginning your defense by using Joe is a ballsy start. "Not that I know of," Sere said.

"They won't. Not until they have their personally groomed pet."

"And how would you know what the most powerful family in New Orleans is up to? You and your real are gutter punks. If you're bullshitting me again, I'll slice that little head off that scrawny neck."

The girl had the same wide-eyed hungry look of desperation as the street kids who hung around the Scratchy Dog. "After you left hell, rumors about a way out spread. Then the first escapee proved it was possible for even a soulless doppelgänger to make it through hell's gate. When our escaped brothers started reappearing as memoryless drones, however, it wasn't hard to guess someone was sending them back. My contingent was handpicked for this mission. We were told if we killed to not eat the victims' souls when they died—be they our reals or strangers."

The knife felt like an extension of Sere's hand, itching to be thrust into the doppelgirl's throat. "You *eat* their souls?"

"That's how we hide them from the loas of the dead," the

girl said so matter-of-factly that Sere wondered how much of life her real had spent in New Orleans's gutters.

"So what happens to the soul? You just shit it into hell?"

"Do I look like a fucking science major?" the girl said. "How am I supposed to know what happens? I know I don't take shits, but then, I doubt you do either."

"Fine," Sere said in exasperation. "If this recent horde was so well organized, how did *you* end up a part of it?"

"Isn't it obvious? They needed someone who could identify you. Or did you think they were just going to capture anyone who fell into their trap on the highway?"

"So you pointed me out. That is all the more reason for me to end you here and now." Sere edged forward on the dock.

The girl kicked Sere's helmet over to her. "I could have captured you. I didn't. I could still let you enter the cabin and find what my contingent left for you. But I won't. I'm siding with you, and if that means you cut off my head, so be it. I'll return to hell as another mindless drone. But you should know there aren't as many empty shells in hell as there used to be. We're learning that we're *not* our reals. Self-awareness is like a disease, and it's spreading. And in case you didn't already know, you were patient zero."

Sere couldn't help having been the first conscious doppelgänger. Others were responsible for her condition. They'd have to take the blame for the living demons as well.

"Your dimension isn't my problem. At the moment, you are. Your story had better get a hell of a lot more beneficial fast if you want to keep that head on your shoulders."

"I'm telling you all this so you'll believe me. I'm not trying to hide anything." The girl got down on her knees.

"Just distract me while your pack of three head down to the city," Sere said.

"That was a game you lost the minute you headed north instead of standing guard in New Orleans."

Sere knew the girl was right, but that only made her want to slit the doppeldoll's neck all the more. "What do you know about what they intend to do?"

"As you said, I'm just a gutter punk. I only know what they told me. I wasn't to commit any souls to hell, and Devlin was to be taken to New Orleans at all costs."

Sere couldn't afford to waste any more time. Bart would be headed to the cabin at any minute, and if he stepped into the trap, there was no telling how much more time would be consumed saving him. She stood up from her attack stance. "If I don't decapitate you, what am I supposed to do with you?"

"I'm still of use to you. The paranormal wraps you use to access your real have been laid under all of the doormats. One wrong step, and you'll be knocked out. Let me stay here until you get back so you can prove what I'm telling you is true. I promise you, I'm on your side."

If what the girl said was a lie, Sere wasn't about to leave the demon with Joe's arsenal. A large wave rocked the dock just before a loud thud from the bottom announced the return of her beloved alligator. "Lefty! Good boy."

The giant gator lifted his head from the river and set it on the dock like a rowboat pulled partway out of the water. He had her shotgun gently cradled between his open massive jaws. Not a tooth mark could be seen on the wooden butt.

Sere grabbed the waterlogged weapon. Though it was useless, she aimed it at the girl. "This animal from hell is my friend. He'll take you to a cabin deep in the swamp. Behave, and he won't eat you."

The girl leaned forward on her knees and patted the monster on the head as if he were a little bunny. "He's so cute. I've never had a pet before."

Sere's exasperation got the better of her. "He's not *yours*, and he's not a *pet*. He's a ferocious demon-eating monster, and you'd be wise not to forget it." Lefty rolled onto his back in the river and offered up his scaly chin to be scratched by the girl. "You are not helping, mister," Sere yelled.

The little demon rubbed the gator's massive jaw. "He's so soft."

Sere couldn't take any more. "Do what I want, and he'll let you play with him. Disobey me, and he'll chew you up like a doppelgänger-shaped gummy bear."

The girl turned to face Sere. "Since you are going to let me live and accept my help, would you mind using my name?"

Shit. The only demon who'd escaped hell that Sere addressed by anything other than her list of doppelcurses was Monty, and he'd managed to infect Fisher with his presence. "Fine, what do you want to be called?"

"Doodlebug."

~

SERE WAITED until Lefty had swum the little demon out of sight before turning to Joe's cabin. She still wasn't sure she was doing the right thing by letting the girl live. The sound of Bart's Ducati pulled her attention from what she'd done to what was ahead of her. *I need to see what Joe has for me.*

She ran up to the front of the cabin before Bart had time to bust the door down. Though the paranormal wraps wouldn't have any effect on him, she couldn't be sure those were the only traps the demons had set. "How did it go at the bar?" she asked.

He finished taking off his helmet, gloves, and jacket. "Edie knows what to say to Fisher. He hadn't called when I left. I hope you're right about him figuring out our message."

"How'd she take the news about Joe?" Sere almost hated to ask, but hearing that the barmaid had lost her shit over the man's death might relieve some of the built-up anxiety that sat like a boulder in Sere's stomach. *Someone needs to mourn him.*

Bart shrugged. "Edie has a lot of lovers. She doesn't get close to any of them."

"Joe and Edie were *not* lovers." The words came out of Sere like an accusation.

"Look, she was sorry to hear about his death. Is that what you want me to say? She hardly knew Joe. Even if they'd had sex, she still would have hardly known him. You can't expect a woman to go all brokenhearted over a passing flirtation."

Sere made a quick assessment of Bart's pants and shirt to make sure conveying the message was all he'd done with

Edie. Though she knew she was being foolish, the memory of seeing him fuck the barmaid wasn't easy to shake. "I suppose you're right, and we really don't have time to discuss Edie's dating habits. Joe's cabin is booby-trapped, but it shouldn't affect you. Once you're in the door, pull the rug up and disconnect the bandage. I need to grab whatever it was that Joe left for me, then we need to get down to New Orleans."

He gave her a sideways stare. "So you were just hanging out here, getting some early-morning sun, while you waited for me?"

"Nope. I've been dealing with that remaining doppelwhore that escaped our grasp."

Bart frowned and nodded. "That was a woman? Interesting. I don't see any demon gore on you."

"I let her live."

He leaned back against the side of his motorcycle as though she'd hit him with a stun gun. "For the love of God, why?"

"She convinced me she was still of some use. If she isn't, simply extinguishing her will be too good for her. I'll take my time to make sure she suffers physically the way I'm suffering emotionally."

"Remind me not to get on your bad side." He opened the door and pulled out the strip of cloth with two fingers as if it were a dog's pee rag.

Walking into Joe's cabin was even more emotionally wrenching than straddling his motorcycle. "Why is it so cold in here?" Sere rubbed her arms.

Bart opened the sliding glass door at the back of the

room and disposed of the second paranormal trap. "That's probably your reaction to Joe's death. People experience loss in different ways. Though it could also be the result of these hidden cloths."

I don't have time for this emotional nonsense. Sere headed for the bedroom while doing her best to ignore the hurricane of emotions that swirled within her. After pushing the small bed out of the way, she pulled up the loose floorboard. Between the joists was a black leather satchel with her name embossed in gold on the front. She sat on the bed, opened the bag, and pulled out an envelope with her name on it.

If you're reading this, I must be dead. That means you're probably also in trouble, so I'll dispense with the emotional baggage. In this briefcase, you'll find information on all of my worldly possessions. They're yours now. I've also included letters of recommendations and introductions to anyone I thought might be helpful to you. Use them wisely. If your destination is New Orleans, I'd recommend starting with former Chief of Police Gerald Laroque. You'll need to follow my instructions about reaching out to him. Though his loyalty is to his sister, he's not about to let the world burn down on her account. In case I didn't get a chance to tell you, I'm proud of you and always have been.

"Fuck you, Joe." She stashed the page back in the envelope and closed up the satchel.

Bart peeked in the doorway. "Did you say something?"

She blinked back the tears and waved at the soft-leather briefcase. "Just another mission from Joe."

Bart sat close beside her. "We've been rushing around since the moment he died. I know discussing emotions isn't your strong suit, and even losing people you barely know weighs heavy on you. Joe was so much more than just a mentor."

She casually brushed her hand over her eyes to wipe away the tears that threatened to gush out of her. "You're not helping."

"I just want you to know you're not alone. I could never fill the hole Joe left, and I'm not trying to." He put his arm around her shoulders. "But I am here for you. I'm not going anywhere."

I can't deal with this right now. Instinctually, she leaned against his side, wishing she were able to explore the emotional connection he was opening to her. "I need your skills, knowledge, and strength more than ever. You have to realize how vulnerable that makes me and how much I *hate* being dependent on anyone." She pulled out of his embrace, got up, and grabbed the satchel. "We need to get riding. First, I need to swing through Myers to exchange that Blackbird for my Triton."

He nodded as if understanding her need for action to tap down the flood of emotions that threatened to drown her. "Yep. That high-performance bike isn't going to do you much good in stealthy operations if everyone knows about it. Plus, it won't work worth crap in stop-and-go traffic."

She breathed a little easier at being able to refocus on the job ahead, even though a part of her wished they could snuggle on the bed all day and see where their emotions took them. What she really needed was some time to think. "You should head on down to the city. We need to find out what Fisher is up to. My detour won't take long, and we can't afford to waste any more time."

Though she didn't want to keep anything from Bart, it seemed unwise to share her plans with him. Setting up a meeting with a member of the presumed enemy's family—and one who'd been in charge of the city's police department at that—was something he might object to.

12

Like a creature of the night returning to its lair, Sere pulled the Blackbird into Madeline's garage just as the first rays of dawn cast shades of yellow and orange on the wispy clouds high overhead. Her snakes were lounging on the gator-skin saddlebags strapped to the Triton like two old men on a front porch with nothing better to do. She couldn't believe it had only been thirty-six hours since she'd ridden out with Joe. Off in the corner, his old BSA motorcycle sat like a relic destined for a museum.

She rolled the Blackbird to the back of the garage next to the antique and threw the black tarp over it like a mourning veil. "I suppose it's now up to me to put Joe's equipment to good use." Though she couldn't come up with an immediate need for the speed demon, the bike's stealth and power were far too useful for it to sit unused for long.

She was back on her Triton with her shotgun and snakes

before she realized Madeline should be told about Joe. "Fuck." She looked down at the snakes with their heads sticking out of the saddlebags. "I just can't deal with talking to a civilian at this point." Reasoning that the condolence would probably take all day and the demons wouldn't wait, she fired up the bike, headed out the door, and clicked the remote to seal up the cache.

After she'd been busting ass up and down the swamp highway on the Blackbird, the old café racer felt like a city scooter. She appreciated the change of pace. Both snakes kept their heads poked out of the saddlebags with their forked tongues flicking the breeze like little kids holding spinners out a car's windows. Being on the road, moving at a sane speed, gave her time to think.

Demons had once again invaded her reality. Joe was dead. The most powerful family in New Orleans was attempting to copy her immortality. Yet with none of those issues pressing down on her for immediate action, all she could think about was Rampart "Bart" Thibodaux.

She could handle an attraction that was purely physical. Bart was certainly a fine specimen of human masculinity. Such walking sculptures weren't unknown in the hell she'd grown up in. Back then, all she needed to do was grab the doppeltoy by the belt buckle and have her way with it. Bart, however, had his own soul, desires, and emotions that prevented her from living out her carnal urges. She could rely on her memories of sexual escapades to defuse the longings, but the emotional availability he'd shown her wasn't something she knew how to deal with.

So far, she'd relied on the idea that he'd infected her with his blood and soul, creating an impure desire in her—one that wasn't natural. As long as she was the only one experiencing the emotion, it remained little more than a crush she could analyze away. Watching him fuck Edie while imagining it was her was close enough to how Sere had dealt with doppelgängers for her to find the sexual play between the two real people mildly amusing—well, perhaps more than mildly.

"Why the hell did you have to sit next to me while I was still emotionally raw from Joe's death?" That simple act had touched her soul as no action of a man ever had before.

She was relieved to pull off at the exit Joe had indicated in his instructions and turn into the abandoned gas station. "This place would have made so much more sense for hiding those high-performance motorcycles."

Joe must have had his reasons for imposing on the quiet neighborhood and, worse, the innocent old woman. Sere swung her Triton behind the old station. The phone booth had been so covered in graffiti that it was hard to imagine the receiver could be lifted from the cradle without first being cut loose from the spray paint. "Where did you find these places?"

She kept the Triton running while she reached over from the bike to the pay phone. Though there wasn't a dial tone, she pressed the buttons Joe had written down.

"Hello." The male voice on the other end had no emotion.

"Joe's dead." She didn't know what else to say. Though

Joe had given instructions on how to reach out, he hadn't left some secret password to prove she was worthy of the meeting.

"Take the streetcar to City Park. Find the old girl scout camp by the lake. He'll meet you at dusk." A quick dial tone followed by silence indicated the conversation had ended.

She looked up into the brightening sky. "That should give me just enough time to rally the troops."

SERE PULLED up to the offices of Montgomery Fisher, CPA and double parked in front of the door. "I won't be long," she said to her snakes.

The little slithery dudes rolled around in the saddlebags so fast the gator skin looked about to come alive. Madeline kept her property so clean the reptiles probably hadn't even found a single field mouse to chase.

"I'm sorry you guys were bored in that garage. I promise, the next place I stop I'll find you something to eat." Sere didn't bother taking off her shotgun. Hiding her activities from Linda had gone on long enough. If the old woman hadn't yet figured out that CPA stood as much for Ceaseless Poltergeist Annihilators as it did for Certified Public Accountants, that wasn't Sere's problem.

She pushed open the door. "Is he in?"

The haggard receptionist slid an envelope across her desk to Sere. "This is not how a professional business is run: people who barge in here without appointments, a worker who shows up when she darn well pleases, and an owner who seems to think his receptionist can juggle all of the requests like a circus freak. I'm *going* to be asking for a raise if this keeps up."

Sere opened the flap and pulled out the hastily written page.

Meet us at the warehouse. You know which one. The gang's all here, including a mad guard dog. We're just waiting for you.

Bart

Sere stashed the note in her pants pocket. "Thanks, Linda."

The exasperated woman held up a half dozen notes. "And what am I supposed to do about these requests?"

"I'll see that Mr. Fisher is in the office bright and early tomorrow."

"You'd better."

Sere stepped out of the office, feeling like a dental patient who'd just learned that she needed a root canal. The combination of meeting place and the term *mad guard dog* had to indicate that Fisher had again apprehended the professor's old lab assistant Thomas. Having been forced to swallow a shotgun pellet, the man was likely more demonically insane than ever, but it wasn't the little nemesis that worried her. *The gang* had to mean Kendell and her contingent. Bart and Fisher were always content with letting Sere take the lead. The people who'd raised her in hell, however, still viewed her as a child who needed protecting.

"I don't have time for interpersonal politics." She kicked

the motorcycle engine over and headed through the city streets toward the warehouse along the Industrial Canal.

SERE PULLED between Fisher's parked Jeep and Bart's Ducati. She reached in her saddlebags and let her snakes coil up her arms for moral support. "Once we get inside, don't go slithering too far away. I may need you to help me make an impression and maybe even give some moral support."

As she marched in the front door, everyone turned toward her. Her stomach quivered at seeing Bart's smile, which extended from his kissable lips to the lines beside his soulful brown eyes.

"Glad to see you made it," he said.

Before her emotions got the better of her and she said something in front of the others that she might regret, her attention turned to the middle of the crowd. Thomas lay thrashing on the floor like a wild animal caught in a snare. Ropes were tied around his arms and legs. His eyes had turned completely red. Drool ran from the sides of his mouth.

"What do you want from me now?" he growled.

She wasn't sure. Instead responding to him, she turned to Fisher. "Don't get me wrong. I'm glad we're not worrying about him causing mischief again, but what were you thinking?"

The CPA superhero sidekick in his seersucker suit pulled on the leash as if trying to get the mad dog to heel.

"You told me to take charge while you were away. After I talked to Edie, I figured you'd want to get everyone together. This seemed to be the most secluded place to meet, but I found demon boy camped out in the office."

Bart must have caught her look of concern. "Fisher called from a burner phone."

Fisher smiled at her look of confusion. "I've got a stash of them at the office. Not all of my clients are on the up-and-up. It makes them feel better if they know our conversations are confidential."

"In case I haven't mentioned it lately," she said, "I'm damn glad you agreed to be my partner in the city."

He held up the leash. "This was just my most recent activity. Before capturing Thomas, I tracked down every bank transaction within a ten-mile radius of Bart's bar. Those demons are getting clever. I didn't find a single illegal transaction."

Sere shrugged. "It doesn't matter. We know three of them snuck past us and found their way to New Orleans."

Fisher shook his head. "Oh, I found the little buggers, even though the person in charge did a fine job of covering their tracks. Not many people can make money appear out of thin air. There's always a corresponding bank account somewhere that records the debit—or in this case, thousands of accounts losing miniscule interest payments."

Once again, Sere was amazed at Fisher's financial forensic abilities. "What did you find?"

"The money came from Marjory Laroque. She's the only one powerful enough to manipulate that many bank accounts. The cash was distributed to moneylending shops from Jackson's Bluff to New Orleans like a trail of cheese for the rats to follow. My guess is she didn't know where the demons would surface, so she spread a wide financial net. I've been tracking when and where the money's been collected. Between their bar stops and unexplained delay outside the city, they've only been in New Orleans for six hours."

Sere felt hope building in her chest. If Marjory had only had her new toy for a few hours, it was unlikely she'd managed the soul transfer. Such things took time, and impetuousness was never an attribute of the bank president.

No ONE HAD MENTIONED Joe. Sere assumed Bart figured she would want to break the bad news herself. The others deserved to hear it from someone he loved. "Their delay was to booby-trap Joe's cabin." She wrapped her snakes over her shoulders for support. "I haven't been around real people enough to know how to say this, and it's not like it was something you'd taught me to deal with growing up. So here it is: Joe's dead."

The soul-sucking silence in the warehouse made Sere wish she'd chosen other words, though she couldn't imagine what they would have been. In slow motion, Kendell put her hand to her mouth. "How?"

"He was saving me. Instead of calling out for my help, he lay quietly dying so I wouldn't rush into an ambush. By the time Bart and I got to him, he only had minutes left to live."

Bart put his arm around Sere's waist. Though she knew

she should reject his compassion, her knees went wobbly as she leaned against his side.

"There wasn't anything we could have done even if we'd gotten there earlier," he said. "Joe's injuries were too severe. He only hung on long enough to say goodbye."

Sere appreciated Bart's support, but showing weakness wasn't going to help her remain in charge of the group. She straightened up and took a half step out of his embrace. "So we're down our main military strategist, and we know our enemy has possession of the three demons. What other issues are we dealing with?"

Kendell crossed her arms over her stomach as if she were about to be sick. "We can't find Sanguine. I've checked every source I have, short of reopening the interdimensional gates we formed to keep an eye on Baron Malveaux. She should have responded. Without talking to her first, I don't dare try to close the gate to hell like you asked."

Sere wondered why she had to be the one to disclose all of the bad news. "I talked with her." Again, the stunned silence pulled at Sere's soul. "The demons conducted an experiment on me. The details aren't important at the moment." From the stern look on Polly's face, Sere knew that not everyone shared that assessment. "My consciousness traveled back along the power line to hell or, more specifically, the devil's old interdimensional iron cabinet. Someone in hell abducted Sanguine and is holding her prisoner there. She believes the doppelgängers are able to escape because she isn't exactly in hell, but she's still close enough to power up the gate. It's as if our hidden foe is using her to prop the door open."

Polly put her hands behind her back and started pacing the way the professor did when working out a problem. "Sounds like we have a lot to discuss with the professor."

"It'll have to wait," Sere said. "Sanguine is okay for the moment. They're not going to hurt her, and it turns out the demons aren't out to kill me. They need us both. She's one end of the power connection, and I'm like the electrical cord into life. The demon explained that their survival in this realm is based on the residual energy from hell that comes off me."

Polly nodded as she paced. "Then the most obvious answer to ending them would be to throw the switch, but that would also end your existence. Other than that, we could send you back to hell, but that might not even be possible now that you have Bart's blood in you."

"Polly Urethane," Kendell yelled, "don't even talk like those things are options."

Polly stopped walking. "Of course they're not options, but a scientist has to consider everything, even if it isn't reasonable. I'm just trying to see our situation from the demons' perspective."

"Stop it, both of you." Sere said. "This isn't the time. The Laroque family has three demons, and from what I've seen, I believe one of them is a Laroque doppelgänger. I've concluded they want to transfer the soul of the real person into the immortal demon body." She pointed at Thomas, who had calmed down at hearing the new information. "We already know what happens when a real and a doppelgänger share the same human body."

Fisher smirked. "Possession doesn't *always* result in the demon side taking charge."

"Fair point," Sere said. "But with both you and Thomas, we're talking about two sides of the same being struggling for control within *human* bodies. A member of the Laroque dynasty might embrace having evil at their beck and call, especially if it meant living forever."

Polly was pacing again. "Such a union might also be an attempt at bypassing the interdimensional power cord that keeps you going, or rather, creating a personal connection to hell. Basically, they're cutting our umbilical cord."

Kendell shook her head in apparent disbelief. "I will never understand why our family is so intent on creating a devil."

Myles wrapped his arm around Kendell's waist. The show of affection and support that came so naturally to the couple after two decades together nearly brought tears to Sere's eyes. Bart had a similar ease with taking command of her emotions, but the fear of becoming reliant on his support kept making her pull away. Kendell, however, didn't show the slightest bit of the submission that Sere had dreaded as she accepted Myles's love and support.

I've got so much to learn about relationships, Sere thought.

"The question," Myles said, "is how do we stop them? And if we can't, how do we rid the world of another megalomaniac intent on ruling over every human being? So far, our exorcisms have relied on voodoo, and if we're going to keep the loas of the dead out of the picture, we can't approach their religion."

Sere hunched down and studied Thomas, who mentally hovered between sane and demonic. "While you all debate the inner workings of paranormal spirituality, I'd rather focus on the problem directly in front of us. Bart, do you still have the med kit Joe gave you?"

"Of course. It's in the storage bag on my Ducati. Why?"

She looked up at Polly. "During the demon's experiment, they forced me to swallow a shotgun pellet. By coiling up the bandage, we were able to draw it out from my gut. Maybe we could do the same thing for Thomas."

"Won't work," Polly said. "Even using the bandage as a magnet requires a connection to a real. Since Thomas isn't a doppelgänger, there's no one to connect him to."

"What if I wrap the cloth around my arm?" Sere asked. "Since I don't need Jennifer's healing power, I won't absorb the energy. I can be a paranormal electromagnet."

Polly shrugged. "I suppose it's worth a try. Worst case is nothing will happen. What do you hope to accomplish?"

Sere turned back to Thomas. "He's worse off with the pellet in him. You said it would magnify whatever power was in charge. Maybe the pellet will do more than that. It's hell based, as is his demonic possession."

"I think I see where you're going," Bart said. "If the demon is holding onto the pellet, it might get pulled out as well." He headed out to the motorcycles at a slow jog.

Polly looked over her shoulder at the retreating muscular bartender. "That man is smarter than he looks. And he looks damn fine."

~

POLLY LAID the bandage over Sere's palm then wove it up her arm like a trainer preparing a boxer for a fight. "I hate to be the voice of optimism, but assuming this does work, it might be a good idea to have a plan for the demonic spirit. If you're correct about Thomas's demon being locked onto that pellet, he'll be searching for another host once he's out of that body. You're a doppelgänger, so it's unlikely it'll be coming after you."

Sere hadn't considered that she might be putting Jennifer in danger. "What do you have in mind?"

Polly turned to Kendell. "You wouldn't happen to have any spirit jars left in the VW, would you?"

"Of course. I keep a couple on hand at all times."

Sere stared at Kendell. "You just carry voodoo jars around like an old woman with hand sanitizer in her purse?"

"Since I'm dealing with the voodoo equivalent of a little girl who keeps scraping her knees, it seems like a good idea." Kendell headed toward the door without waiting for a response.

Sere wondered if the woman would ever see her as a grown-up rather than thinking of her as a child who kept getting into trouble.

Polly connected the power line to the bandage around Sere's hand. "It would be best if you didn't get too close to Jennifer during this exorcism."

"From my experience, the pellet takes a bit of time to work its way out of the body, so I'll be able to warn Jennifer to keep away before the demon surfaces."

As soon as Kendell returned with the square blue-glass jar, Polly held up the med kit's cell phone. "So here's the plan. I'll be outside running the connection. Once I power Sere up, Thomas is going to be thrashing around like a madman. Myles, Fisher, and Bart will need to hold him down. No matter what happens to Sere, do not touch her. When the pellet is out of Thomas, Kendell will scrape it off Sere's bandage and into the spirit jar. Do not touch the pellet. If it falls, let Sere pick it up again with her bandaged hand. Only when it's safely isolated and capped in the voodoo jar will I turn off the connection. We can't risk Thomas's demon breaking free to possess the first human he comes across."

SERE PUT her hand on the man's stomach like an old-time faith healer. *At least I don't need an incantation,* she thought. "Ready?"

Thomas's eyes were still wild with demonic anger, but his clenched teeth proved he was struggling against the urge to fight back. He gave her a single nod.

"Hit it," Sere called out to Polly.

The itchy tingling sensation of the elastic bandage turned into pulses of electricity that ran from hand to elbow. Sere's muscles flexed as if they'd just been supercharged. The body under her touch writhed with demonic fury. "Hang in there, Thomas."

Bart had hold of the man's feet while Myles and Fisher

held each arm out as if nailing Thomas to a cross. The constant struggling, combined with the power that surged through Sere, nearly made her forget about Jennifer. Like a photograph that had been double exposed, Sere could make out the ghostly image of the homemaker working in her kitchen overlaid on the scene in the warehouse.

"Stay back, Jennifer." Though Sere spoke the words out loud in the warehouse, the woman at the stove looked in the direction of the struggle on the concrete floor.

"What's going on?" Jennifer's words sounded as ethereal as she appeared. No one other than Sere looked in her direction.

Sere had never witnessed their connection from outside of Jennifer's body. "We're performing an exorcism. I needed to borrow your energy. Just give me a minute, and we'll let you be. Whatever you do, don't come any closer to me."

"I'm not afraid," Jennifer said.

"I am," Sere responded, crouched under the woman's kitchen table.

A black hole lined in fire tore the fabric that separated their two realities. Between keeping her hand planted on the bucking, demonically possessed Thomas in life, maintaining her cool despite the flames of paranormal energy running up her arm in Jennifer's imagined kitchen, and making sure the woman didn't become another of the possessed, Sere felt like a juggler who couldn't afford a single distraction.

The demon who walked through the gap between dimensions and materialized in the homemaker's cheerfully decorated domain, however, made Sere want to turn and run. Twice Thomas's size, covered in blood, and snarling like a rabid dog, the creature turned first to Jennifer and then to Sere. "Release me," it roared.

"What in the name of all that's holy is that?" Jennifer yelled through the roaring flames.

"A resident of hell." Sere got out from under the table then stood to face the demon.

Once the monster was fully through the gap, Sere felt a tug on her arm from in the warehouse. *For the love of God, Kendell, don't fucking drop the pellet.* Sere couldn't imagine how she'd be able to find it amid the chaos.

Once Sere pulled her hand off Thomas's chest, the black hole in Jennifer's kitchen closed, releasing the demon into the space between the two women. The monster turned toward the homemaker. *Come on, Kendell, move your ass!* Sere mentally pleaded.

"It won't come off the bandage." Kendell's voice sounded like it came from far down a corridor, not right next to Sere.

"Shut off the connection," Bart yelled.

"No, don't." Fisher's voice sounded much closer. "The demon needs to be contained first."

"What am I supposed to do?" Kendell yelled. "I can't touch the pellet, and the knife just slides right off it."

"Do something before he gets me!" Back in the kitchen, Jennifer's panic radiated into Sere's chest. The creature had clearly zeroed in on his next victim and was moving in to take possession.

"Not so fast, asshole." Sere clenched her fist around the pellet. The demon puffed up in anger but moved no closer to Jennifer. "I can't hold him forever," she called out to the others in the warehouse. "Someone think of something."

"Have them turn up the power," Jennifer yelled from the other side of the demon. "You can crush him like a bug."

"Can't do it," Sere replied. "It would drain you. Our connection only works if I respect the boundaries. Too much of an imbalance between us might cause my soul to infect yours the same way this demon slipped into Thomas."

"Okay, then don't do that," Jennifer said. "But I want to help."

The demon stared at Sere as if she'd just revealed some weakness. Blood dripped from its mouth like saliva. "All I have to do is wait you out. You can't hold me forever." Unable to advance on Jennifer, it moved in closer to Sere. "Or maybe I'll just devour your soul."

The clanking of an iron skillet onto the tile floor made the demon turn to look at what had happened.

"You don't want her," Jennifer said.

Sere strained to focus on Kendell. She didn't dare say aloud what she was thinking for fear the demon would be ready with a counter move. Holding her fist to her chest in front of Kendell, Sere flipped it over as if flipping the switch away from herself.

Kendell nodded, whispered in Fisher's ear, then held the bottle with both hands close to Sere's fist. Fisher gave Sere a quick nod and ran toward Polly, who was standing outside the roll-up door.

Focusing back on the scene in the kitchen, Sere stared into Jennifer's eyes, willing her to understand. With the demon distracted by the homemaker, Sere pointed first at her chest then quickly at Jennifer. Jennifer gave a trembling single nod that Sere mimicked in the warehouse.

"Now," Kendell yelled to Polly.

THE ENERGY REVERSAL sprang Sere's fingers out straight, freeing the pellet from the electromagnet bandage. The willpower and self-confidence she'd relied on no longer made up the bedrock of her existence. She had all the trepidation and terror she had experienced as the scared little girl who'd just been yanked out of Guinee and dumped in hell. Staring at her transparent arm, she realized that with her power now being sent to Jennifer, she was nothing more than a disembodied ghost in the kitchen, unable to confront the demon. She had to test how far the transfer went.

"Hey, asshole, I'm over here," she yelled at the monster. Her voice faltered from lack of conviction.

The demon didn't even flinch. Freed from Sere's grasp, he crept around the butcher-block table like a cat sneaking up on a mouse.

"So this is what it's like to be you," Jennifer said as she picked up the hot skillet from the floor.

"Don't fuck around, woman," Sere yelled to Jennifer. "That demon means business. Just hold him off until Kendell can take the pellet from my hand."

"But until she does, this bastard is mine."

Since the monster hadn't responded to Sere, she assumed only Jennifer was able to hear her. She had to help somehow. "Though you can see him, he doesn't have any mass. He only exists in this energy connection we're sharing. That cast-iron club isn't going to do you any good. Focus on keeping him out of you."

Jennifer raised her hand toward the demon as if she could vaporize him with sheer force of will. He continued circling around the table toward her.

"I thought you said he was nothing more than energy," she said.

"He's been trapped in a body for the last twenty years," Sere said, "and before that, he had substance in hell. If you try to hit him and have your attempt go straight through his body, he'll learn quickly that he doesn't need to navigate around your kitchen." She could feel the woman's desire for combat growing.

Jennifer backed toward the sink like she was luring him into her trap. "Come on, you bastard. Show me those big demon fangs. I'll bet you just love towering over defenseless humans."

Sere had never seen a battle from the perspective of those she cared about, but listening to Jennifer, she realized the words weren't that different than the taunts she would have used. *Think. Analyze the situation. What would I do? How can I help Jennifer?* Even without her self-confidence, Sere still had Joe's training to rely on.

"I know he looks imposing, but he's kind of a chickenshit. In all the years he was trying to take over Thomas's life, he barely managed any true evil at all. Demons feed on power, and right now, he's losing energy like a toy that had its batteries left on all night. Treat him the way a woman authority figure would deal with a schoolyard bully."

Jennifer straightened her stance and crossed her arms under her breasts, the skillet still in her hand, as if she were about to tell Thomas to go to his room. She shook her head. "You are just so precious. Am I supposed to be afraid of you?"

The creature puffed himself. He had to keep his head bent to fit under the ceiling. "I am a demon from hell, and I'm going to take possession of you, body and soul."

The woman chuckled. "I dressed my son up as Dracula last Halloween. Even he had a better dark accent, and he's only nine."

Sere felt the tongs Kendell had improvised from Bart's knives press into the bandage around her hand. "Time for you to go into your little jar, pesky demon."

The demon evaporated as easily as butter in a hot pan. Jennifer's eyes switched from the monster that had been between them to Sere. "You."

Sere turned her face away. "You're not supposed to be able to see me."

"I got it, Polly," Kendell yelled. "Better call 9-1-1. Thomas doesn't look so good."

With the connection to Jennifer severed, Sere collapsed onto the concrete floor. Her arm stung, but the sensation was now only physical. She rolled to her side and looked in Thomas's eyes for any hint of the demon. They were as crystal blue and pure as a mountain lake.

He lay gasping for breath and bleeding from the hole in

his stomach. "Thank you. I'm finally free. You fulfilled your promise."

DRAINED OF ENERGY, Sere struggled to push herself off the floor. Bart pulled her onto his lap. "Just take it easy for a minute. I've got you."

"It worked." She couldn't quite believe it. Beheading Thomas in hell had been one of her earliest mistakes, though the freed demon taking possession of the real wasn't completely her fault. Professor Yates had used the boy's image as his hell-based assistant. Too many facts rolled around Sere's mind for her to make sense of what had just happened and how it might help with the fight ahead.

Polly knelt down next to her. "You were right about that pellet. It did more than just separate the doppelgänger from the real. You thought it might magnify whatever was already in charge of the body."

Sere did her best to help Polly make sense of what had happened. "Thomas had lost his battle against his demon, so the pellet amplified the evil."

Polly looked over at Fisher while talking to Sere. "And you hoped having your friend swallow one might help him combat his inner demon."

Sere took hold of Polly's arm and pulled herself up from Bart's embrace. "I'm still not willing to use him as a test subject. Fisher isn't the problem—whatever the Laroques are creating is. What would happen if a doppelgänger body —inhabited by both the evil copy and the human spirit—

were to undergo what Thomas just experienced?" Sere's strength ebbed, causing her to fall back against Bart.

"That's an interesting premise." Polly stared at the warehouse ceiling. "A doppelgänger body already connected to its real would bypass the professor's equipment. We'd lose all control over its ability to regenerate, as it would have a self-contained source of energy—basically like running off a battery. A single paranormal pellet inside wouldn't be able to sever the connection, but it would still focus on strengthening the dominant energy. More than one pellet, however, would only confuse the two spirits. As with Thomas, the pellet would need to be inside the body long enough to fully isolate the main source of power. Once the pellet had done its job, it would have to be removed the same way you just did with Thomas. Going in and digging it out would only allow the dominant energy to be reabsorbed by the body."

Sere wasn't crazy about subjecting Jennifer to another demon, but the woman had performed admirably for her first time facing pure evil. With a little training, the happy homemaker might make a formidable ally. "Would it matter which persona was magnified?"

Polly bit her upper lip. "It shouldn't. Disconnecting either one from the body would be like removing either the positive or negative terminal from the battery. Either one would render the toy doll unresponsive. And unlike you, the remaining spirit wouldn't be able to draw on an outside energy source because it's no longer being run through our interdimensional computer."

That explanation made Sere's head swim. She

concentrated on the next step, and her mind cleared. "So we would need a way to inject a single shotgun pellet into the doppelgänger without him noticing."

Bart helped Sere to her feet. "I'm on it." He grabbed a couple of shells from her belt. "Give me half an hour in one of Joe's hidden workshops. There must be one somewhere in this city."

Though she was still weak, she appreciated his no-nonsense attitude. There was work to do. "Grab the black satchel from my saddlebag. There's a map in there of Joe's hidden caches. I'll swing by Fisher's offices once I finish with my meeting."

He leaned in and kissed her on the cheek. "Don't go doing something foolish—at least not without me."

As he left, the paramedic van pulled up. Things were about to get busy, and Sere didn't have the time or skills to come up with a believable excuse for Thomas's injury. She took Kendell's arm. "Help me to the back door." She checked to make sure the rest were dealing with Thomas. "I'm looking for a gutter-punk girl. She's shorter than me, like, five-foot nothing, mid-to-late teens, and scraggly black hair that probably hasn't been washed in a month. She might go by the name Doodlebug, but I wouldn't count on it."

"Is her doppelgänger among the latest outbreak of demons?" Kendell asked.

Sere wasn't ready to let on about the girl out in the swamp. "I received some information, and I'm trying to decide if it's bullshit or worth pursuing."

"I'll see what I can do. If she's in the Quarter, I should be able to find her and bring her by the Scratchy Dog before we open tonight."

"There's no need to alert her just yet. Get a picture so I know you've found the right girl, but just keep track of her for now. Depending on how the information pans out, I might not even need her." If the little doppelchick was lying, having the girl's real at Sere's mercy might prove useful.

13

*S*ere rode her motorcycle back to Mr. Fisher's offices and left it in the care of the homeless who were always camped out in the narrow alleys. Then she ducked into the offices and stripped off her shotgun and holster. From inside the saddlebags that she'd dumped on the chair, her snakes rattled their displeasure.

"I hate leaving you guys again, especially when I'm going somewhere you'd love," she said, "but making a show of strength against this dude probably wouldn't end well."

Even if the former head of the police department wasn't afraid of reptiles, people on streetcars had a way of freaking out when they saw rattlesnakes poking their heads out of women's bags.

Down to just the knife in her boot for protection, she headed out of her office. "Mr. Fisher should be in shortly," she said to Linda. "He wanted to check on a client in the hospital."

The receptionist glared from behind her computer. "He's taking too personal an interest in some of these new customers you've brought in. And I've yet to see an invoice for his services. This isn't how business is conducted."

"So you've told me," Sere said. Though saving the world seemed a reasonable distraction from combing through taxes, the receptionist had a point. Mr. Fisher wasn't going to stay in business long if he was only working part-time. "I promise, once this latest issue is resolved, we'll both round up some paying clients."

Sere had to run the block from the office to Canal Street to catch the City Park streetcar as it clanked to a stop. The old wood, iron, and glass car reminded her of the horse-drawn version she'd ridden as a child. Filled with humans and their associated odors, this one smelled only slightly better than the one she remembered. Once she took a seat on the cramped wooden bench, the car jerked into motion. Between the lurching, claustrophobic confines, and human stench, she wondered if the covertness of leaving her motorcycle behind had been worth the effort.

By the time the streetcar slammed to a halt at the last stop, Sere's legs felt like they belonged to an eighty-year-old woman. She groaned as she unbent her body from the cramped space. *I swear, I'm walking home. Maybe I'll get lucky and someone will try to mug me. I could use the workout.* In spite of the painful ride, she returned the conductor's smile as she stepped off the iron step.

Walking through the park helped calm her nerves after the physical shakedown of the streetcar. The place lacked the wild untamed life of the swamp, but she felt free of the constant bombardment of humanity and their prying eyes—both actual and technological.

It took her a half hour of exploring the hidden trails to stumble across the small cabin made of stone and wood that sat on the bank of a man-made lake. On a park bench by the shore, an old man was tossing bread to the ducks. They huddled around him in the water as if he were a regular benefactor of the flock.

Sere walked through the damp grass toward the man. "Excuse me. I'm supposed to be meeting someone."

The man looked up, his facial features familiar, even if they were hidden by wrinkles. "I'm Gerald Laroque. Have a seat. I've still got half a loaf to work through."

The former chief of police looked like a kindly grandfather more apt to pull coins from behind children's ears than direct cops with batons against rioters. "Thank you for seeing me," Sere said. "Joe recommended I meet with you first."

The old man turned back to his ducks. "I was sorry to hear about Joseph. He was a good man. If it's okay with you, I know the department would like to handle his funeral. Though it's been some time since he was on the force, we do like to take care of our own."

She hadn't even considered what to do with his body. Letting the police take care of the arrangements seemed the most logical answer. "I think he'd like that. Did you know him well?" The connection between her mentor and one of the most powerful members of an evil family had never made much sense to Sere.

"I don't think anyone knew Joseph well. He gave each of

us a puzzle piece of his identity. I relied on him. That's not something I'd say about very many people."

She couldn't afford the time or emotional energy of once again diving into Joe's death. "If you've been his connection in the city, you must know what I'm up against. But how can I trust you?"

The man sat stiffly upright. "Not a bad first question. Together with my sister, we ran the Laroque dynasty and this city—which were really one and the same. That was a long time ago." He hunched back down as if the mantle of power had been too much for him to bear.

"What happened?" she asked, though she wasn't just curious about his past. If there had been a schism within the family, she might learn of his motivations. There had to be something about the man she could trust.

"The shortest answer? Lieutenant Joseph Cazenave. He was such a fucking Boy Scout when he joined the force. If it weren't for the recommendation from a mutual friend in the military, I wouldn't have given Joseph's application a second glance. God, that man had no sense of humor at all. I only put him on paranormal investigations as a joke. Of course, that was before our family learned that the Malveaux curse was real."

"I don't need a rehashing of ancient history."

Gerald turned his glassy gray eyes to her. "By the time my nephew Lincoln went missing, Joseph had told me about your existence—as well as the return of your father. Officially, the department never found the body or the perpetrators. As you can imagine, that didn't go over well with the family, especially my sister. They were trying to oust me from the force when her bank was bombed. My last act as chief was to cover up Joseph's involvement. Without him, there was no way to track down the other miscreants."

She never had been fond of long-winded stories. "But why would you side with him over your own flesh and blood? Especially if you were one of the people in charge of your family dynasty?"

He turned back to his birds as if they might be the only ones who would understand. "When your father returned and took possession of Lincoln, body and soul, a change came over my sister. Being rich and powerful was no longer enough for her. Improving the city and extending our reach didn't matter. Meeting her ancestor in the body of her son was as close to a religious transformation as I've ever witnessed in her. She had a new life's mission."

"Raising the devil," Sere said.

"I may be biased in her favor, but I don't think Marjory realized that what she was seeing in Lincoln was evil. She was witnessing ultimate power: the ability to defy death itself. Money and political influence seemed like kids' board games in comparison to what Lincoln had achieved."

Sere couldn't imagine the rage the woman must have felt when her god had been destroyed. "So she forced you out in retaliation for the loss of her son and god?"

"Officially, yes, but the new chief doesn't concern himself too much with his men. The sergeants and beat cops that I trained are now captains and lieutenants. I may not have the title, but you can bet I've still got the influence."

So that's how Joe managed things, Sere thought. "That's an interesting story, but it doesn't do me much good right now."

He handed her a couple of slices of bread to feed to the ducks. "I wasn't finished. What do you know about the old World Trade Center?"

More history? Really? She tore up the slices and threw them at the birds with such force they swam out of the way of the bread projectiles. "There was some secret organization that kept paranormal artifacts out of the hands of the general public. They had responsibility for handling my father's cursed possessions. They failed, and the organization disappeared without a trace."

"Good enough. They used these iron vaults to secure the items."

Sere squeezed her eyes shut in frustration. "I am familiar with them."

"What you might *not* know is that a couple of them turned up in the Mississippi River. When Marjory had the bank rebuilt, she snagged one and put it in the subbasement. She's been running tests on what your father achieved ever since—much of it based on your existence."

"How the hell does she know so much about me?"

"Throughout his life, Baron Malveaux kept journals. Everything he did in stealing you back from Guinee, as well as his observations about hell, he wrote down. Once you surfaced, Marjory realized the possibility of becoming immortal. You're kind of like her messiah. In you, she sees what humanity might become."

"But those writings would have been while he was *in* hell," Sere said. "How did she get her evil claws on it?"

"Unfortunately, I don't have all the answers. Some things you'll have to find on your own."

"I'm still not sure I should trust you."

He stood and emptied the last of the crumbs from the bag into the lake. "If you did, I'd be wildly disappointed in Joseph for not teaching you better. One last thing…" He crumpled up the bag and tossed it into the garbage can. "I'll tell you what I can and point you in directions I think will help, but I can't get you out of jail or save you from my sister's grasp. Get caught, and you're on your own. And don't come running to me with every little piddly-ass question. I'm only useful if the rest of the family doesn't know what I'm doing. Hit me up too often, and they'll figure it out fast." He turned and walked away like he was about to be late for dinner.

BART WAS WAITING in Sere's office when she returned. "How did your meeting go?"

She had been careful about not mentioning her rendezvous. "Who says I was meeting someone?"

"Linda said you ducked out unarmed. I've never seen you go out in public without some protection, so I assumed you had to be meeting someone. Mind telling me what's going on?"

"I met with former chief of police Gerald Laroque, and before you tell me I was being reckless again, it was Joe's idea." Sere would have preferred not to share that news, but keeping it from Bart would have bitten her in the ass before too long.

To her relief, Bart nodded. "I assumed he had some resource down here. That's quite the confidential informant, though. Did you learn anything useful?"

"I got some good background information and confirmed that the Laroques are responsible for the latest escaped demons. What do you know about breaking into banks?"

"Hey, my background is military, not larceny, though I suppose there may be some overlapping of skills."

She considered confiding in him that Joe had been behind the bank bombing. A little testosterone-driven rivalry might prod Bart into action. But restricting that information to only those involved had kept everyone safe for decades. "Eventually, we'll have to confront our enemies on their own turf."

"I'll look into it. Why is it that as soon as I solve one problem for you, another bigger one is just waiting in the wings?"

"Welcome to my life. So in solving my latest little issue, does that mean you figured out how to inject our human-doppelgänger hybrid with a pellet?"

He pulled a copper shell from his pocket. "This is a hollow-point bullet. They split on impact, creating a large amount of damage. If we use one on our target, our adversaries will assume we tried to blast a hole in the body. As I've learned from watching your supernatural healings, to conduct the repair, they'll first have to dig out all of the metal shards. It'll be messy work. Once they've finished, the body's flesh will seal up." He pulled out a second round that had already been fired, showing the metal flower shape created by the impact. He then dropped a pellet into the small indentation in the center of the spent slug. "What they won't realize is that when the bullet exploded, it injected a paranormal pellet into the doppelgänger's body. They'll be so busy digging out the shell that the real threat that lies deeper in the flesh should go unnoticed."

She patted her four-barrel shotgun that lay on the desk. "There's a reason Joe built this blaster for me. He used to tell me I've got shit for aim, but I stand a chance with this thing. However, a little bullet isn't going to do me any good in a shotgun. How am I ever going to hit a demon with a handgun?"

Bart pulled his .38 special from the back of his pants. "I guess you'll just have to rely on me, then."

Her heart nearly stopped at the idea of Bart putting himself at such a risk. "We're not talking about some random shooting here. Whoever gets the immortal body is going to be someone well positioned in the Laroque family. Between the dynasty's ownership of the police and influence over the media, this isn't going to be the kind of attack to go unnoticed."

"Good thing I'll have a demon-hunting badass to protect me."

"I'm serious. If you shoot this guy, your life won't be worth the spent slug. I can't risk losing you."

"Well, what's your idea? Do you want to bake him a cookie with the pellet inside like a king cake with the hidden plastic baby Jesus?"

She hated it when he had a point. "No. Like me, the doppelgänger body won't have to eat, and even if he did, he'd sense the paranormal energy like the smell of a rotting fish on a platter."

Bart leaned over the desk and took her hands. "Exactly. He can't know that he's been infected. I'm really very good at shooting people, though this may be the first time in my life that a woman has seen that as a *good* thing. You have to trust me."

She stared into his captivating dark-brown eyes. "So long as you don't expect to do this alone." If she looked at him one more moment, she'd be pulling him across the desk to have her way with him. Instead, she broke eye contact, picked up the shotgun from the desk, and leaned it against the wall. "If we can only infect him with one pellet, there's not much point in me constantly hauling that thing around. Joe always warned me not to see it as a crutch. Though their paranormal medic would undoubtedly dig every pellet out of his flesh, they would also be on the lookout for any strays in other parts of his body. Shooting him would only alert them to our plan."

Bart leaned back in his chair. The lines around his eyes indicated her lust hadn't gone unnoticed and might well have been reciprocated. "How's your sword play?"

"It's been a lot of years since I handled a long blade. Joe tried teaching me, but eventually, he didn't see much point in training me to use such an obvious weapon."

"Any idea why he would keep a couple of katana swords in his cache?"

She remembered the feel of the braided leather handle.

"Those must have been the ones we trained with when I was a girl in hell. They would be fitting. That's what I used to decapitate Thomas's doppelgänger."

Bart handed over the black satchel. "Joe worked up a comfortable little hidden workshop in the ninth ward. If you're not planning to lug that shotgun around, we'll need to outfit you with new weapons. I can take you there if you like."

The prospect of being alone with Bart in a place where they wouldn't be discovered had her heart beating harder than she thought possible.

14

Sere led Bart on a spirited cat-and-mouse motorcycle chase through the Bywater neighborhood. Once she was sure they weren't being followed, she doubled back toward the bridge over the Industrial Canal. As they crossed the man-made river, she settled in behind him for the respectably reverent ride along the deserted streets of the Ninth Ward.

The tires of her Triton slipped in a mud-filled pothole as Bart made a sharp turn onto a narrow path as if he were riding a dirt bike. Once off the street, the lack of pavement made for a smoother ride between the brush and tall grass. Though not far from the main road, the 1960s-era bungalow at the end of the dirt driveway was well hidden by dense vegetation.

"This is it." Bart removed his helmet. "Not the easiest place to find. My first time here, I had to double back three times to spot the turnoff. I can't imagine how Joe stumbled across these places for his caches."

She stepped off her bike and listened for any hint of neighbors. Only the songbirds and crickets greeted their arrival. "Joe once told me the police knew every drug den, gang hangout, and secret sex club within the city limits. Being on the force, once he busted one of the establishments, he erased the location's existence from the database and set up his hidden cache. How he found the spots outside of the city, however, is anyone's guess."

Bart put his hand on the small of her back. "If this is too emotional for you, I can slip in and round up some weapons."

With its peeling white paint on the vinyl siding and weathered blue trim so cracked the wood barely hung onto the nails, the place looked like it hadn't seen an occupant since Hurricane Katrina.

"I already know Joe's ghost has moved beyond this world. If there is any living thing in this place, it will only provide me with a good workout." She pulled open the ratty screen and twisted the handle of the half-rotted plywood door. A stench composed of mildewed carpet, rodent droppings, and death made her retreat into Bart's arms.

"Give it a minute," he said, grabbing her by the hips to steady her. "The good news is the smell is only in the front room and kitchen. It must have been his way of dissuading trespassers. Once you get down the hallway to the master bedroom, you'll hardly notice it."

She had trouble believing the smell could be so easily contained, but trusting Bart, she held her nose and ran to the far end of the house and through the bedroom door. The moment Bart also passed the threshold, she slammed the door on the stench. She waited until he took his hand from his face and took a breath before following his lead.

"Not one of his subtler booby traps," she said.

"Maybe not, but it is effective." Bart took hold of the sagging mattress and lifted. A hidden hinge along one side and pneumatic actuator on the other held the bed up as if it were the hood of a car. Rather than box springs, an arsenal of guns, knives, and swords lay neatly organized in the hidden weapons locker.

The upturned mattress was so close to Sere's face that she couldn't help but breathe in the smell. Unlike the rest of the house, which made her eyes water in pain, Joe's aroma of Irish Spring soap and Gillette deodorant over the deeper notes of his body odor brought emotional tears to her eyes. "How do you continue fighting for what's right when you know you could die at any minute? What is the point to life if it's so transient?" Her question, based in frustration, wasn't meant just for Bart but also the great beyond, where Joe might still be listening.

"I live for today and try not to think about what comes next. Maybe some people would take that philosophy and live a life of decadence, but I find helping people far more fulfilling." Bart pulled the two katana swords from under the bed. "And when I start getting melancholy about my fate, I find a good workout session refocuses my attention." He aimed one of the handles at her.

Immortality meant Sere literally had all the time in the world, but that wasn't the case for those she cared about. To them, every day would be precious, and she'd wasted enough of Bart's time with her unexpressed emotions and desires. She walked up to him, took both swords from his hands, and tossed them on the ground. "I've got a better idea." Wrapping her arms around his shoulders, she pressed her body fully to his. As she stretched up to her tiptoes to bring her lips to his, she felt the bulge in his leather pants against her waist grow larger as if his cock was helping pull her up.

His hands clasped her butt cheeks so fully and forcefully it felt like she was being strapped into a carnival ride. He lifted her off her feet until their foreheads pressed together. "It's about fucking time."

She breathed in his hot breath as if it were a drug. Her legs wound around his waist like boa constrictors and pressed against his rock-hard ass. With him supporting her weight, her hands were free to rip his skintight T-shirt from his back. She ran her hands lustily over his chest.

He ground his throbbing cock against her in time with his breathing. "You're not the only one with a wild side. I want you so bad I could tear your clothes off with my teeth."

With one hand, she let go of his body and pushed the mattress back down over the weapons cabinet. She then leaned into him as if hunching down over her motorcycle before accelerating to full speed.

Instead of collapsing to the bed, he slowly sat back like a young oak tree bending in the wind. His legs flexed so large and hard between hers that she felt even more like she was back straddling the dangerous Blackbird motorcycle. Once he fully settled onto the mattress, she arched up from him and lifted off her leather halter top. Her nipples tingled as if his eyes were teasing the tips.

His hands explored her body from butt to breasts until his palms completely covered her small mounds, leaving only her light-pink nipples protruding from his grasp. Rip-cord strong, his fingers twisted her tender flesh.

She grabbed his hands and pressed them hard against her boobs. Her hips ground against him as if trying to rub their pants away from their mutual longing. *Why the hell don't pants come off easier?* she thought through her endorphin-filled haze of desire. Her fingers quivered as she traced every muscular curve of his arms.

With each flexing of his hands against her breasts, the cord-like tendons in his arms adjusted under her touch like the taut strings of a musical instrument. She leaned forward into his grasp as her hands descended from his arms to his chest. She hadn't realized she'd closed her eyes until she opened them. He stared back at her with his longing-filled smoky-brown eyes.

I could spend a lifetime gazing into those pools of dark amber, she thought.

As her hands worked down his rippled stomach, his left her breasts and caressed the curves of her sides. They met at the tops of their motorcycle riding pants. As she fumbled with his belt, he unclasped the snaps and the concealed zipper of her pants as if he'd designed the damn things. She barely had his buckle unlatched when he snaked his hands under her leathers, grasped her by the cotton-panty-covered hips, and flipped her to the bed.

"That's not fair," she protested.

Kneeling on the mattress, he gave her clothing one firm tug, yanking her pants and panties down her legs and off her feet and pulling her boots off with them. He tossed the pile of clothing on the floor like discarded wrapping paper before towering over her. "I thought you might want a better view for your first time seeing a real man."

"I'm not a virgin," she said as much to her longing as to his taunt. She lay mesmerized as he finished unbuttoning the top of his pants and worked the zipper down. From under his boxer shorts, his cock looked to be doubling in size now that it was free from the leather confines. When he pulled down his shorts, she realized how naïve she'd been in thinking she knew anything at all about men's bodies. Doppelgänger cocks looked like little plastic doll willies compared to his towering rock-hard shaft that arched out at her. Veined, dark tan, and throbbing, Rampart's cock lived up to every one of her fantasies. Saliva filled her mouth as it bobbed in front of her face like a thick nine-inch finger beckoning her closer.

"My turn." She bolted up so fast she head butted him in the chest as she grabbed his body. With her hands around his ass and his cock between her breasts, she nearly lost focus on the fact that there were still clothes to remove. She flipped him sideways on the bed then ran her hands along the dimpled sides of his butt, along the leg muscles that dwarfed her palms, and finally, to the pants and shorts bunched at his thighs. With a couple of grunting pulls, she had the last of the clothing off his magnificent Adonis-like body. She saddled up to him, grasped his cock, and lowered her pussy onto it.

He ran his hands up her thighs. "You don't mess around, do you?" he asked as his cock throbbed into her.

Her hips began their usual rocking action that she'd used on the doppeldildos in hell. "I suppose I'm used to taking charge of my sexual needs." Talking about what she was doing had never been a part of her release. She grabbed the sides of his abdomen, closed her eyes, and humped his cock.

Instead of just lying there, he sat up and wrapped his arms around her waist. "Try to relax a little. Take it slow. Sex isn't a battle. It's a collaboration of desires. Let me show you." He leaned his forehead against hers. They sat facing each other with her legs around him and his cock inside her. "See how our breathing has synchronized?"

She wasn't looking for collaboration. Sex was about the release of frustrated desires. As she stopped trying to dominate him, though, her body developed a rhythm with his. His cock gently explored parts of her she'd never felt before. And as her body began to accept the foreign presence, so did her soul.

Unlike her previous psychic mergings with human spirits, she remained fully herself in her own body and Bart in his. Yet there was a connection between them. She could anticipate each movement of his hands on her hips, his head pressed to hers, and his cock against her clit. Each of her body's movements found him at the ready like a dancer prepared to lift her desires higher into the air. The synergy magnified her longing to keep him inside her.

Okay, big boy, show me what you've got. Once she stopped forcing the action, he started working his cock like a conductor directing an orchestra: circling, thrusting, gently retreating then plunging hard. And like a performer, she submitted to his every gesture, allowing the desire to build like music within her.

At her orgasmic crescendo, he maintained a thrust so deep inside her she found it hard to breathe. Every part of her, body and soul, quivered against him. She held her hands tightly to his shoulders and pressed her head so hard to his she feared she might bruise him. Her rock-hard nipples teased along his chest until their sensitivity rivaled that of her clit against his cock.

As she trembled down from her orgasm, he grasped her butt so firmly she could feel the building undulation rolling through every part of him. His gave a low grunt of animal desire from inside his clenched jaws, then his inflated chest crushed her breasts. His six-pack abs rippled against her stomach, his hips forced against hers, and finally, his straining cock exploded deep within her. His hands pulled her hard and close as his magnificent body shook against her like an earthquake that had its origin in his soul. His warmth filled her so completely she felt as if she would burst. Spent, he lowered his head to her shoulder.

She wove her fingers into his wiry black hair and gently cradled his head to hers. Flexing her butt cheeks, she held him within her for as long as she could, but his drained cock lost its rigidity almost as fast as his tired muscles. Slowly, she eased off of her body's tight hold around his cock. "Why does it have to be over?"

He put a finger under her chin and lifted her lips to his. "So we can do it again from the beginning." His passionate kiss was quickly followed by his muscles flexing their readiness for another round.

THE BARE MATTRESS over the weapons locker was only slightly less comfortable than the one in Sere's loft, but being stretched out naked next to Bart was closer to heaven than she'd ever hoped to experience in this or any other lifetime. As she lay with her head on his shoulder, she ran her fingers through the sparse hair on his chest. With her leg arched up over him, his cock throbbed valiantly against her inner thigh. The man was exhausted. She'd ridden him like a racehorse, and even thoroughbreds needed a break after winning the Triple Crown. Gently, she rubbed his cock with her leg to express her appreciation without trying to rile it up again.

His massive hand gently caressed her sweaty hair. "Who are you, Sere Mal-Laurette? You're not like any woman I've ever met or hope to meet. Where do you come from?"

Sere hadn't shared her personal history with anyone and wasn't sure she was ready to start. "It's a long, complicated story, and you don't really want to hear it."

He turned slightly on the bed and moved his hand from her head to her back. The adjusted position allowed her to slip her leg between his, causing his cock to extend along her thigh to her hip. "I want to know all about you. This is what people do after making love—they share their most intimate life stories."

She flexed her thigh, hoping the stimulation to his cock

would distract him from his inquiry. If he had enough energy to listen to two hundred years of nonsense, he'd hopefully prefer to refocus that energy back to having sex. "It's really not as interesting as you might think. I'm more a live-in-the-here-and-now kind of woman than a let-me-unburden-my-past-trauma type."

"You know I'm not going to let this go. We're more than partners, at least as far as I'm concerned. Sex was the physical part of our new status. Confiding in me is the emotional end."

Fuck you, Bart. Refraining from snarkiness, she said, "Okay. But I'm telling you, it's a lot of information—more than most people would be willing to endure. So any time you've had enough, just say so, and we can go back to fucking."

He kissed her on the forehead before snuggling her again in his python-like arms. "*Boring* is not a term I will ever use to describe you. Lay it on me."

She rested her head against his chest and wrapped her arm around his abs while their legs remained woven together. "I guess to understand me, you'd first have to see my father as I do. He wasn't always the devil, but he never was a good man. By the time I was born, he was already the bank president, which made him the most powerful man in New Orleans. He used that position to ruin anyone who crossed him and more than a few who didn't. He took whatever he fancied: men's wives, daughters, land—whatever his opponent cherished." She pressed her cheek hard to his muscular chest. "But even that wasn't enough for him."

"This is the part that I've never heard explained. How did a powerful man extend his reach beyond the living?"

"With the help of a voodoo queen, the first Mardi Gras parade, and the stealing of a loa of the dead's source of power. Baron Samedi was the most arrogant of the loas of the dead. He never could say no to a good party. So when my father and Marie Laveau concocted a celebration of New Orleans to honor the loas, the old fart couldn't resist participating. The loa actually thought he could show up incognito. That's when my father took his cane and control of the seventh gate to Guinee. Bad as Archibald Malveaux was as bank president, his evil took on a whole new level of malevolence once he became ruler of the afterlife and took on the title of Baron Malveaux."

Bart resumed caressing Sere's head, but this time, the action felt less stimulating and more comforting. "Is that when you committed suicide?"

Sere sighed. "Even that's complicated. One of the men my father ruined—Kendell's multi-great grandfather—paid to have a curse cast on my family. I was the first to fall under its power. I did slit my wrists with my father's knife, but a six-year-old girl can't really muster the strength to cut through tissue with a small, dull blade." She arched her neck to face Bart. "Remember that knife. It was just a little thing my father used to clean his pipe. It'll come back later in my story."

"Noted," Bart said with a smile.

She settled back against him. Unburdening herself of her story was a bit like drinking: the more she shared, the more addictive it became. "My soul landed in Guinee. With my father in charge, that version of purgatory was filled with women and brothels. Instead of passing souls through to the *deep waters* like he was supposed to, he selectively hung onto those who suited his desires. This is where my personal journey pauses. What I know of what happened next with my father comes from more of those family stories Kendell made me suffer through as a child. She had this conviction that I needed to know everything she'd done. I still think she looks to me for some sort of validation."

"She loves you," Bart said offhandedly.

"I don't know what that means, and even if I did, it's unimportant to the story. When my father finally did die, his soul took up residence in Guinee as the most powerful loa of the dead—guardian of the seventh gate, which during life he'd positioned in his office at the bank." She looked back up at Bart again. "This is another important point, especially considering our current disaster."

He nodded without interrupting her.

She settled back into her story and against Bart's chest. "You'd have thought being in control of every dead soul would have been enough for the asshole, and for one hundred and fifty years, it was. But when Kendell stumbled across the pipe tool in an antique store, the old goat started getting ideas of returning to the land of the living with his immortal powers."

"Kendell doesn't impress me as the type to collect antiques," Bart said.

"She's not. Myles had some harebrained idea that he could see past events by holding onto objects. It turned out he was more right than he knew. Apparently, Kendell and Myles had met in college. They took a class together about paranormal energy transfer. Bet you can't guess who taught the seminar."

Bart's fingers curled against Sere's head. "Don't tell me. That whack-job professor out on the docks who runs hell's computer simulation."

"Very good. A-plus. But I'm getting ahead of the story."

Bart laughed and patted her butt. "For a badass, you can be a real nerd at times."

She pinched his chest in playful retaliation. "Anyway, the more Kendell and Myles fucked around, learning about the curse and falling in love, the more my father found ways of manipulating his way back into life. He finally took possession of Myles. It didn't last long. With a little help, Kendell was able to perform an exorcism and forced my father's spirit into a voodoo totem."

"Why didn't the story end there?" Bart asked.

"It should have, but this is the point where we meet some of our current enemies. I already told you a little about the Laroque family. Through careful breeding they developed a worthy successor to my father: Lincoln Laroque. As Marjory's son, Lincoln had every advantage money and breeding could achieve. She even named him Lincoln in an attempt to make his Southern roots more palatable to the general United States population. She intended on him becoming president, but he had loftier plans. The arrogant prick drank the spirit jar containing my father's energy in an attempt to surpass his ancestor."

Bart's stomach muscles tightened. "Wait. He *voluntarily* submitted to being possessed?"

"One thing you should know about the Laroque family—their arrogance knows no bounds. Lincoln thought he could control my father. Of course, it ended up being the other way around. Since you were just a kid at the time, you probably weren't aware of when Baron Malveaux returned to run the bank. Marjory and her brother Gerald were able to keep the more sensational aspects of the *new* bank president out of the press." Sere pushed against Bart's chest, laying him flat on the uncomfortable bed. She then rolled on top of him to press against his cock and rest her breasts against his chest. "Are you tired of my story yet?"

He put his hands behind his head as if offering up his body to her. "Not at all. Feels like we're just getting to the good part."

"The complicated part maybe. I've never told you about my guardian angel. Sanguine Delarosa was a swamp witch and granddaughter of Agnes Delarosa. I've got Doodlebug sequestered in their old cabin. Hell's version of that beat-up shack is where I was raised, but that comes later.

"Anyway, when my father took over as the seventh loa of the dead, the voodoo queen realized the mistake she'd made, but as he was now the leader of her religion, there wasn't much she could do to fix the situation. She and Agnes—then a young swamp witch with the gift of foresight—formed a partnership. They both realized the day would come when the devil would need a cage."

"You mean hell?" Bart asked.

"Exactly. For the rest of her life, Agnes devoted herself to creating the alternate dimension. From every brick in every building in New Orleans clear out to every blade of grass in the bayou, the old swamp witch made an exact duplicate of this reality. But it was still only a blank canvas devoid of human beings." Sere crossed her hands over Bart's chest and rested her chin on them. "You know, on its own, that realm isn't half bad."

"What happened next?" Bart asked.

"Like the voodoo queen and the old swamp witch, Kendell and Sanguine realized it was up to them to stop my father, who was now reincarnated as Lincoln Laroque. Together with their friends, they managed to cast the old goat into Agnes's creation."

Bart frowned. "But how did we end up with doppelgängers in hell?"

"Did you really think after ruling life and death that something as mundane as a hell dimension could contain the devil? My father kept finding ways to manipulate hell in an attempt to escape." Sere thumbed Bart on the chest. "Remember that bit about Myles seeing past events in inanimate objects?"

"Sure."

"Well, Kendell's Scooby gang got this bright idea that if my father *thought* he'd escaped, maybe he'd settle into his new domain and leave them alone. But they had another problem to contend with. That stupid pipe tool ended up in a paranormal collection of my father's things. Some dipshit organization thought it was their responsibility to contain magical objects. My father found their vaults in the abandoned World Trade Center building. In one of his efforts to escape, he set off a paranormal nuclear meltdown in the facility. Left unchecked, the runaway energy would rip a hole between all three dimensions: hell, life, and Guinee. He also managed to steal the magical vault containing his possessions.

"This is where the professor stepped in. His invention uses every structural part of New Orleans to record the activities of the people who inhabit the city. According to Kendell, the old scientist had speculated on the possibility of inanimate objects being used as recording devices during the class he taught. By using the power from the paranormal nuclear meltdown, his equipment transferred that information into Agnes Delarosa's world. Using everything from her bricks to her blades of grass, the professor's data is projected into hell, which is what creates the doppelgängers. In theory, those puppets are just supposed to be mimicking what their reals are doing."

"I'm guessing something went wrong," Bart said.

"Yep. Me. The doppelgänger puppets weren't meant to see one of their own develop consciousness."

"I was just wondering when you were going to resurface in your story."

The memories made her wince. "Even hell dimensions have rules, and as this one was designed to mesh with voodoo traditions, seven gates needed to be created along with seven guardians to look after things. Sanguine had her spot out in the swamp, Myles the courtyard behind the Scratchy Dog—you get the idea."

"I thought we were getting back to you." Bart said.

"I'm Kendell's biggest single mistake. You remember how my father's office was the seventh gate to Guinee?"

"I *am* following along, Sere."

"Okay. Well, Kendell got the bright idea that I should be a gate guardian. Kind of a give-the-devil-his-due type of situation. Because I was dead, they used the old office as the gate so I could be contacted in Guinee. Time in the afterlife can be a fucked-up mess when it comes to interdimensional gates. In my time line, I'd only been dead a few days when Kendell contacted me through the newly reinstated Baron Samedi. God, I still hate that loa."

Bart gripped Sere's shoulders like he was about to toss her out of harm's way. "*Kendell* is responsible for you being made into a doppelgänger?"

"Indirectly, though she really should have known better than to tempt my father with my soul like that. Using the interdimensional vault that he stole, his cursed personal possessions, and my blood, which was left caked on the pipe tool, father was able to yank me through the gate. He'd already abducted Jennifer's six-year-old doppelgänger and put her in the magical box. And there you have me: Sere the soul inhabiting Jennifer the doppelgänger. I was to be the devil's first immortal. He had the audacity to think he could continue stealing the souls of the recently deceased from the loas and create his own dimension filled with those who would bow down to him."

"But your father is no longer in hell, is he?" Bart asked.

"Papa Ghede—the watcher of the seven loas of the dead—offered his help to Myles. His intention was to return my stolen soul back to Guinee, but Kendell and Sanguine had other ideas. Instead of slipping me through the gates and back to Guinee, they captured my father and dragged him to the *deep waters*. That's why the loas are such a threat to me. They believe there's a soul left in hell: my father. If they found out that they were duped and *I'm* the one still free of their grasp, they'll come after me. And if they find that I'm not in hell, they'll tear this world apart looking for me. They can be pretty single-minded when it comes to escaped spirits."

"What about the bank explosion and the special shotgun shells?"

Sere leaned forward over his chest, laid a passionate kiss on his succulent lips, and closed her legs around his growing erection. "That's another story. Now, show me what other interesting things you can do with that cock."

DAWN WAS JUST BREAKING when they left the run-down house. Sere had never felt more genuinely human. Her body tingled from head to toe. "I don't want you to get a big head, but that sex was pretty amazing."

Bart had his arm around her waist. "Right back at ya."

It wasn't exactly the response she'd hoped for. "Even better than Edie, Riley, or any of the other bimbos you take to bed?"

"Not even close. I only had sex with those women out of boredom."

She looked up at him, wondering how close his

experiences with women had been to hers with doppelgängers. "And you don't feel bad about that?"

"Why should I? They used me every bit as much as I did them. There was nothing emotional or romantic about our encounters."

"And what about us?" Sere asked, wondering if it was possible for someone to have a true emotional connection with her. She was, after all, physically more doll than human.

The lines around his eyes straightened into a harsh stare. "With all of your abilities to connect to people, do you really have to ask? Of course what we just had was emotional—more than that. I'm not going to bullshit you and say I've never experienced anything like it before, but this wasn't some quick fuck just to get it out of the way. You and I were bonded before sex. What we just did only confirmed that connection. If you expect some idealized wine, chocolates, and roses type of romance out of me, though, I'm afraid you're going to be wildly disappointed."

She didn't know what she expected. "Well, if you think I'm going to be some little whore who spreads her legs for you every time you flash those dimples, you're the one who's going to be wildly disappointed." She regretted the outburst the moment it was out of her mouth.

"I sometimes forget how limited your experience is with being in love."

"Who said anything about being in love?" she demanded.

He leaned on the seat of his motorcycle and pulled her between his legs. His half-bent position brought him down to her eye line. "I did. I only have two emotional settings when it comes to sex: casual and serious. There is no in-between for me. You can throw all the snarky rejoinders at me that you want, but deep down, I know you feel the same."

She didn't like having the emotional spotlight illuminating her soul. "If you were so attracted to me, why did you wait until I made the first move? I thought alpha males went after what they wanted."

"I tried to, but each time I got close, you pulled away." His hands felt warm and comforting on her hips. "It isn't like we've had a lot of free time together. Besides, I was afraid any overt seduction might be misinterpreted, and I didn't want to get stabbed in the gut just for making a pass."

He had a point. Even in hell, where she'd been able to direct the actions of the doppelgänger cock dolls, she'd never allowed one to have the leading role. She ran her hands over her arms, wishing she were still naked on the bed with his hands exploring her body. Being outside with the cool fall breeze on her skin only highlighted that it wasn't really *her* body.

"I suppose I wouldn't have trusted any man who tried something sexual with this body."

He pulled her so close she had to put her hands on his chest for balance. "Are you worried that I might somehow be attracted to Jennifer's body? Don't be. Here's the way I see it. You're damn good with that knife in your boot, but I've seen you use my combat blade with equal skill. It's not about the weapon. It's about the person wielding it."

She ran her hands up his chest to his neck, wondering if she could be as spiritually pure with her desires. "Maybe so, but you have to admit that having a long stiff blade helps get the job done."

His laughter forced his cock against her. "Using the right tool always helps."

She looked into the brightening sky. "Much as I'd love to spend all day in bed with you, we've got a new devil to stop. Kendell and Myles will be cleaning up the Scratchy Dog from last night's revelry. That seems as good a place as any to rendezvous."

"I'll call Fisher to let him know to meet us on the road."

*A*s Sere stood inside the door of the Scratchy Dog, she was certain that both Kendell and Myles knew simply by looking at her that she'd just had the best and only real sex of her life. Even if they couldn't figure it out from her blush—one of the true disadvantages of being stuck in a redhead's body with its pale-pink flesh that registered every embarrassment like a flashing billboard—they would be able to read the body language. Bart stood so close to her that she could feel the heat radiating from his crotch.

"I need a drink."

"I'll join you," Bart said. "We can keep an eye on each other's intake."

Fighting companions, sexual partners, and now drinking buddies—if this isn't love, I can't imagine how we could be any closer, Sere thought as she headed to the bar with Bart's hand at the small of her back. She took her usual spot at the end of the counter, where she could keep an eye on the room.

Myles pulled out two glasses and the bottle of Jameson's whiskey. "I've grown accustomed to serving Sere any time of the day or night, so I don't ask when she wants a shot before breakfast. But isn't it a little early in the day for you?"

Bart straddled the stool beside Sere. He looked out of place on the customer's side of the bar. "Hanging with her has turned my world upside down. I'll take a Jack and Coke."

Fisher came out of the back room and slid onto the chair next to Bart. From the moisture on his face, he looked like he'd been trying to get himself together after a long night. "Make mine a Sazerac."

Myles finished the three drinks then poured a glass of white wine for Kendell and grabbed an Abita for himself. "Sounds like none of us got any sleep last night."

Sere could feel her blush building as she caught Bart's secretive downcast wink in her direction. She used the excuse of looking past him at Fisher to hide her longing glance in Bart's direction. "What kept you up?"

"Thomas didn't make it."

"What?" Sere nearly dropped her drink. "The hole didn't look that bad. Did I clip some vital organ pulling the pellet out?"

Fisher downed half of the strong cocktail in one gulp. "The doctors didn't have an explanation. He just faded out. They resuscitated him numerous times, but in the end, it was as if he didn't *want* to come back."

Sere could see that Fisher was struggling. Though the

treatment wasn't geared for his situation, the fact that there were the beginnings of a potential cure must have given him room for optimism. Now that one straw of hope had failed.

"You stayed with him all night?"

"Most of the night. I spent the last few hours searching for any relatives he might have who'd want to hear of his death. Apparently, he'd alienated everyone he once knew." Fisher looked down the bar at her. "The last thing he said was for me to convey his thanks. He died as himself and not a demon. Hopefully, that will carry some weight with the loas of the dead."

"I'll see to it that it does," Myles said. "I've still got some pull with Papa Ghede. He owes me for escorting Sere's father to the *deep waters*, even if he doesn't realize it was the devil and not Sere."

Knowing Myles was chummy with the loas was a bit like knowing a family member had voted for the repressive political party in the last election. Sere didn't want anyone to discuss Myles's connection to the loas, ever. Even so, as Fisher straightened his back from the bar, she could see how Myles's offer to smooth the way for Thomas's soul had lifted the possessed man's gloom.

"If he didn't die from his injuries, what do you think happened?" she asked.

Fisher turned the glass tumbler between his hands as if the rapidly diminishing alcohol could warm his spirit through his palms. "His soul was shredded. The demon had been a part of him for so long that the two had fused. Once that evil was pulled out of him, Thomas didn't have anything in this life to hold onto."

"You have us," Sere said, "and your family."

Myles mixed another Sazerac for Fisher. "Not to mention you've done a damn fine job of combating the evil within you. Thomas gave in to it."

Fisher held the glass out to Myles with both hands like a beggar accepting change. "Thomas had to deal with the desires for much longer, and he was just a boy when he was possessed. He never really stood a chance. Even if he had survived the exorcism, he probably would have ended up living on the street. I looked into his finances. For the last decade, his primary source of income was petty theft. I don't doubt that dying free of his evil double came as a relief to him."

Sere realized she probably should have been checking on Fisher's condition. After having sex with Bart, she had a new sense of how self-centered she'd been with those around her. "How are you doing?"

He held up the refilled glass as if reconsidering his need for a bender so early in the day. "I'd assess my condition as stable. There are times, like now, when the temptation to dive into the darkness is strong, but I've got too much to live for." He looked again at Sere. "Not least of which is being your superhero sidekick. So what's the next challenge?"

Sere was glad to get back to forming a plan. Offering sympathy never came naturally to her. "No matter how I look at it, eventually, we're going to need to get into that bank. That's where Marjory will be building her devil like Doctor Frankenstein in his laboratory."

"Assuming they haven't already," Bart said.

At least sex hasn't dulled your edge, she thought as she smiled at him. A partner wasn't much use if he didn't challenge her. "I'd like to say I'd have felt it if they had, but detecting fellow doppelgängers has never been one of my strengths. If we can stop the melding of human spirit into doppelgänger body, great. If it's already happened, I'm betting they'll keep their creation in hiding until they're ready to use him against me."

"I wish we had Joe," Kendell said from behind the bar. She turned to Sere. "I'm sorry if that sounded insensitive."

Sere downed the rest of her Jameson. "It wasn't. We're at a big disadvantage without him. Because it seems pertinent, would you mind explaining how you got in to bomb the old bank in the first place? Interdimensional travel seems like a breeze compared to breaking through a wall of reinforced concrete."

"That was all Joe," Myles said. "We always knew he had his resources. I suppose it made sense to keep his different forces secret from each other. He rounded up a militia, snuck us into the bank, set the explosive devices, and got everyone out before all hell broke loose. We were just there to secure the gate between dimensions. Any time we asked about how he did things, he'd brush off the question with the single word: 'compartmentalization.'"

Sere put her hand on Bart's arm, remembering how it felt as they lay naked together only a few hours before. "You wouldn't happen to have a secret militia hidden somewhere, would you?" *Other than the one in your pants,* she nearly said out loud.

He smiled down at her, indicating that he'd caught her

look of lust. "Sorry. Ex-special-forces guys like Joe are more legend than fact. Even those of us who value our service maintain a break between civilian life and being out on patrol."

Fisher pushed his half-empty glass aside. "Give me a day or two, and remind me to send a bouquet of flowers to my wife. Looks like I won't be home tonight."

"You'd better send a second bouquet to Linda," Sere said. "She's a little pissed that neither of us has reported to work on a regular basis. And what exactly would you know about planning a bank heist? I thought you were completely legit." Though Fisher had pulled off some impressive feats of financial legerdemain in the past, Sere couldn't imagine how studying receipts was going to get them into the most secure room in New Orleans, and they really didn't have time to waste.

"I am," he said. "That's why people hire me, including those who skate a little too close to the legal edge. No one wants to go to prison for tax evasion. It's just not a sexy crime. But calling up one of my more nefarious clients won't be my starting point. As a rich person, Marjory Laroque is as paranoid as they come. In fact, I'd bet a part of her was happy the old bank got bombed. It gave her the opportunity to build something far more secretive."

Bart nodded. "From my experience, highly classified installations never use just one architect. It's kind of like Joe's explanation of compartmentalizing his assets. The less any one person knows, the less they're a threat of spilling the beans. Most of them probably didn't even know what they were working on."

"She wouldn't have used the bank's money for the build," Fisher said. "That would only point fingers at whichever contractors she hired. I'll have to do some digging to discover how she arranged payments, but people are creatures of habit. If I trace back the accounts she used to fund the latest batch of demons, I might find the hidden sources of cash she tapped to fund the bank build. Once I find out who she hired and when she paid them, I know of someone who might be able to reverse engineer the construction."

"I'm still not getting it," Sere said. "A contractor is a contractor. Unless you intend to strong-arm them into divulging what they did or break into their offices to steal their plans, how is knowing who poured the concrete going to help us?"

Fisher smiled at her and winked. "This is why you have me as your superhero sidekick. Everyone in New Orleans specializes. One concrete-pouring company might be good at laying up two-foot-wide walls and curing them so they don't crack during settling, while another might be better at constructing forms for secret passages. Once I combine that information with architects who similarly specialize, cost of materials—which will indicate how much concrete was used—and the timing of payments, I'll have enough data to take to my source."

"But knowing what Mrs. Laroque *might* have built isn't going to get us into that building," Bart said. "We're going to need specifics."

"That's where my source comes into play," Fisher said. "As Sere indicated, breaking into offices to steal plans would only tip our hand. Most construction firms, however, don't spend a lot of time vetting their day laborers. A contractor's disposable employee to my source is like a discarded invoice to me."

"I worked construction one summer," Myles said. "Workers like the ones you describe are impossible to find once the job's complete. To use your metaphor, it'd be like searching for a faded cash-register receipt under twenty years of garbage."

"That anonymity is what contractors count on," Fisher said. "And uncovering the connections is where my source excels."

"I'm almost afraid to ask," Bart said, "but what does your *source* specialize in?"

Fisher smiled. "I only do the man's taxes."

Sere took Bart's empty glass and turned it over on top of her smaller glass. "So for the time being, our adversary will be toiling away in the lab while Fisher figures out their layout." She nodded at Bart's pants pocket. "Show them what you showed me..." She hastily added, "In Fisher's offices."

He pulled out the hollow-point bullet and the spent shell then made his explanation of how he could infect whoever Marjory created with the paranormal pellet. Before returning the slugs to his pocket, he gave her a quick smile that spoke directly to her lusts.

Sere nodded down the bar at Kendell. "Anything to report on what we're dealing with in hell?"

Kendell helped herself to another glass of chardonnay. "Without being able to contact Sanguine, I'm afraid most of what we found is more theoretical than practical." She pulled out a blank receipt from under the bar, along with a pen, and wrote *hell* and *life* on it. "You started off here in hell." She drew a curving line to life. "Made it back here." She drew an *S* next to hell with another line to Sere in life. "And Sanguine is being used to power you."

"Stop telling me what I already know." Sere didn't have the patience for another of Kendell's longwinded explanations.

"This is important, Sere. Whoever is running the show is trying to create another bridge, but until they do, they have to rely on the energy from hell that sustains you to power their construction project." She turned back to her drawing. "When a demon kills a human, the soul is dragged to hell, but that's not where it belongs, so an energy current is created back to life. Ultimately, the soul is being called by the loas, but those guardians of Guinee can't enter hell."

Sere tapped her foot in irritation against the bar. "Again, old news. I did live in the hell dimension, if you'll remember."

Kendell tapped the pen against the bar, looking equally frustrated. "So the trapped soul is like tossing a rock in a river so someone can walk across." She drew little circles between life and hell. "It's only stable enough, however, for a demon without a soul to pass over on it. Here's where things might prove more interesting for you. The demon has to *die* in life and go back to hell to establish the connection. They become planks laid over the rocks." She drew the return line over the circles with such force that she tore the paper.

Sere looked at the crude drawing with renewed interest. "They've been *planning* on me killing the escaped demons?"

"According to the paranormal science, that's how they're stitching together the various planks into a bridge strong enough to support a living human soul."

"I guess I was wrong about the whole one-demon-to-one-dead-person scenario," Sere said. She'd never been comfortable being the one looked to for answers.

"Right and wrong." Kendell shrugged. "So long as they are just laying the planks, they'd only trust one demon to the one human-soul stone in the water. Once they have the bridge built, though, they should be able to use it as much as they like. And seeing as how this latest batch of demons hasn't gone on a killing spree, it would be safe to assume they have enough planks for their bridge."

Sere took the pen and drew three lines that didn't return to hell. "Since it looks like Marjory has selected a doppelgänger to perform her first test in creating an immortal, we have to assume that the demons we just killed up north completed her bridge, leaving these three."

"If Marjory has finished her bridge, why is she limiting the number of demons allowed through?" Fisher asked. "She could call forth an entire horde to deal with us while she performs her tests in peace."

"Crossing over is just the first part," Myles said. "Each of those demons has a will of its own and would need to be powered up for as long as they're in this dimension. A mad rush to this side would overload the power cord. Building an immortal would require all of the energy that connection could handle."

Bart picked up the pen and drew a broken line between the two realms. "What if a demon wasn't sent back?"

Kendell shrugged. "The bridge wouldn't be as strong as our enemies think it is. The missing doppelgänger would be like a loose thread: pull on it, and the whole structure comes apart. But you'd be left with a demon among the living and an obvious missing link that Marjory would be sure to notice. She could just clip the thread. And if Sere is right, they have two guardian demons here in New Orleans that they could kill to create replacement planks."

"We might be able to fool them," Sere said. "Did you have any luck finding that gutter-punk girl?"

Kendell pulled a piece of paper out from under the cash drawer under the bar. "She hangs out with a group that camps on Esplanade's neutral ground. When she arrived in New Orleans two years ago, she went by Doodlebug. Now she calls herself Dooly Buell, but I'm not sure if that's her real name. I couldn't find out where she came from. She plays a pretty decent fiddle. Her current boyfriend fancies himself a poet. I've got my homeless friends keeping an eye on her. Now, would you mind telling me what your interest is in the girl? Because for the life of me, I can't figure out what she has to do with anything."

"Her doppelgänger is the one who killed Joe. I'm keeping the demon alive for information. Lefty has his eyes on her out in my old cabin. If she does anything suspicious, he'll munch her for lunch."

Myles tossed his empty beer bottle in the trash with such force the metal can tipped slightly. "What could she have possibly said that kept you from killing her the moment you saw her?"

Sere appreciated his expression of anger. She still wasn't sure she'd done the right thing in not killing the doppelbitch. "She explained to me that the murdering doppelgängers eat the souls of those they kill. That's how they steal the spirits from the loas and send them to hell. I know for a fact that she did *not* eat Joe. I didn't let the girl live out of mercy. If anything she says doesn't prove true, I'll take great delight in running my knife through that delicate young neck."

"And if what she says does prove true?" Kendell asked. "I'm not crazy about the idea of you keeping a demon like a pet. That thirty-foot gator of yours is enough of a problem."

"Lefty is *not* a pet." Sere couldn't understand people's desire to subjugate every creature they found.

"You know what I'm saying." Kendell's parental tone of irritation sounded exactly like Sere's long-dead mother.

Sere stared at the bar in order to stay focused on her developing idea without being distracted. "We need a way to keep track of what our adversaries are up to in hell. We know I can't go back. If I tried, I'd just end up in the interdimensional prison with Sanguine. Though you and Myles have moved between dimensions with your gates and his voodoo-loa cane, opening up that kettle of undead fish again will only call forth the loas of the dead. We're running out of options. I'm not just leaving Sanguine to languish in that iron box. Eventually, we have to get ahead of this slow-rolling demon invasion, and I'm not seeing that happen by only using the professor's toys. Having our own spy in hell could prove useful. To keep it secret from our adversaries, we need a link to hell that's not part of the professor's software."

Bart put his hand on her back. "And you think having both the real Dooly and her doppelgänger Doodlebug will help create that bridge? Because so far, having a real meet their doppelgänger has been considered a really bad idea."

"And you're not sending that girl to hell in place of her doppelgänger." Kendell spoke with such force that Sere moved closer to Bart for protection.

"I never said anything about sending Dooly to hell." Sere did her best not to yell. "If Doodlebug is going to be any use to us, I need her to return to hell of her own free will. She's not going to agree, however, unless I can promise to bring her back. My connection to Jennifer has gotten me out of some bad situations. Maybe Polly and the professor can work up a similar lifeline for Doodlebug. This time, though, the wrapping would go on the real Dooly to send additional power to hell's Doodlebug."

"Do you really think she'd do it?" Bart asked. "Seems like she worked awfully hard to escape."

"I know convincing Doodlebug won't be easy. The girl I met in the swamp has a lot of spirit. If that's coming from her real, they both might be willing to listen. However, if it turns out that Doodlegänger's spunk is simply from living in hell, there's not much point in letting her live. We'll need both the real person and hell's copy for this to work. If we can send Doodlebug back through the gate, we'll end up with both a spy and an undetected thread we can pull on to dismantle our enemy's bridge."

Kendell collected the glasses. "It might be better if you let me approach Dooly Buell. You can be a little direct at times, and I do have a relationship with the homeless population. They'll vouch for me. Once I gauge her level of willingness, you can deal with her doppelgänger."

Though Sere knew Kendell was right, she had wanted to meet the girl to determine how close the real Dooly was to her demon double. The frustration of inaction made her eager to get out of the bar. "So Fisher will work on reverse engineering the bank plans, and Kendell will see about getting Dooly to the professor for a paranormal fitting." She turned to Bart. "That leaves you with me. I'm done pussyfooting around Marjory Laroque." She got up and headed for the door before the rest could offer their objections.

16

"What the hell are you doing, Sere?" Bart yelled from behind her as she stormed down Chartres Street toward the bank.

"I'm done fighting from the shadows. It's time I had a chat with my distant niece."

"You can't honestly expect to fight your way into the bank president's office." He grabbed her by the arm and swung her toward him. "Think, Sere. She knows who you are."

"She's not going to kill me. She can't. She needs me. I certainly hope this new level of concern for my safety isn't the result of us having sex."

Bart straightened up. "I'll march beside you into hell, and you know it. I'm only asking that you consider the outcome of confronting Marjory Laroque on her own turf. You'll end up in one of those damn iron cages she has under the bank, just like your guardian angel in hell. You'd be walking right into her hands."

"Shit." Sere pulled her arm out of his grasp and kicked the lamppost. "I can't just sit around, waiting for her to make the next move."

"Do you want to go back to Joe's romantic hideaway?" he asked. The smirk on his face let her know he was only half kidding.

"Don't try humor on me when I'm in the mood for battle. There must be something I can do. Every minute, it feels like they're getting one step closer to raising a new devil."

Bart sat on a wooden stoop. "Talk this out with me. What are they missing? Supposedly, they have the doppelgänger body and a human to go in it. They also have a paranormal bridge to hell strong enough to send that human soul to hell and back. If your information from Gerald Laroque is correct, they have the interdimensional iron cabinet in which to conduct the transfer. Having the supplies and laboratory equipment, however, doesn't mean they know how to make the experiment work."

She sat so close to him that their hips pressed together. "Gerald said his sister does have some of my father's writings. It'd probably be too optimistic to hope she doesn't have the one titled "How to Create an Immortal," but reading what my father did and being able to reproduce the project successfully could be very different. Marjory is working in life, and Baron Malveaux did his creating in hell."

Bart casually put his arm around her waist. "I was never

much good at science in school, but I'd guess if Marjory wasn't sure of what she was doing, she'd take things slow and methodical."

Sere nodded. "She hasn't had the doppelgänger body for very long. I think we can assume that she hasn't yet raised a devil. Once she does, if he's anything like me, he'll still need to be powered from hell. The bridge Kendell talked about could also be used as the power cord. Even though it's Marjory's creation, it would still need to be plugged into the professor's equipment to draw on the energy from hell. That means there must be someone helping her who understands what the professor created."

That was about as much as she intended to share with him. Even considering how close Sere felt to Bart, some information—such as how Sanguine had opened the portal between dimensions and provided Sere's connection to hell's power supply—was too dangerous to entrust to him.

"Why not just feed off of your connection the way the demons do?" Bart asked.

"Marjory is one controlling bitch, and I can't imagine that a devil she creates would be any less calculating. The demons might survive as annoying parasites sucking off my power cord, but a true devil would never accept such a limitation."

"Sounds like Polly and Professor Yates's domain."

Sere got up then started pacing in front of Bart while she talked. "Marjory would know better than to try to sneak something through the professor's equipment on this side. Between him and Polly, there's someone there all day every day, so creeping in and uploading a computer virus would be pretty difficult."

Bart leaned forward on the stair. "She'd need someone intimately associated with the doppelgängers' survival mechanism. There can't be more than a handful of people that the professor has worked with over the years. Shit, I've seen the equipment—even used it to heal you—and I don't have the first clue as to how it works."

Sere reached over her shoulders to the twin katana swords strapped to her back under her leather jacket, wishing she could do battle that instant. "How could I be so stupid? The asset Marjory needs isn't in this life. He's in hell. I knew I should have decapitated that little pipsqueak the moment he showed up in the swamp—fucking artificial Andy. He's been conscious in hell since the day I decapitated Thomas. The little creep even knows how to move between dimensions, although he was hooked to a paranormal tether at the time."

"You lost me."

Sere pointed to the gun behind Bart's back. "He's the professor's assistant in the alternate dimension. He's the one who made the paranormal shotgun shells and brought them to me through hell's gate. The little runt isn't supposed to be anything more than a doppelpuppet the professor can manipulate for work in hell's laboratory. But it's becoming clearer to me with each new demon that the professor has lost control of his creation."

Bart flexed his magnificent arms. His bulging tendons reminded Sere of how her breasts had tingled when he worked his powerful fingers against her flesh. "What do you have against the professor's assistants?" he asked. "First Thomas and now Andy. Each time you talk about them, you level up on your intense hatred."

The artificial boys made Sere's skin crawl, but she resisted her revulsion to keep the conversation from careening from helpful to hate-filled venting. "They aren't human, and they aren't doppelgänger. I have no problem dismembering demons, but I do sympathize with them. Any consciousness subjected to the tortures of hell is sure to become distorted. The demons who've escaped have found the only way out of their eternal damnation. What I do is mercy killing. Even if they regenerate in hell, it's without the memories of what they've endured. But beings like Andy have no connections to others. Though they are basically doppelgängers, the professor gave them enough self-will to break free from their reals' lives. They're morally and spiritually blank."

Bart had put his hand up to stop her after she said, "mercy killing," but she'd kept going, needing to get the idea out while she was on a roll.

"But a regenerated doppelgänger must endure the suffering all over again," he said. "How is that a kindness?"

"They lose the memories of the original torment. Hell is hell. Though it may be my inheritance, I've yet to figure out how to make it into a paradise." Sere stopped pacing. "You may not have been much good at science, but it wasn't even offered during my hell schooling. I think it's time we put a little more pressure on the professor."

∾

SERE NEARLY PUT her hand through the cardboard-covered glass door as she pushed her way into the professor's office. "How do we shut down Andy?" She wasn't in the mood for pleasantries.

The old man behind the desk looked even more haggard than the last time Sere had stopped by. "I've told you before, I can't just turn off specific doppelgängers." He waved at his wall of computers. "There's no on-off switch for each person. It would be like asking God to remove an individual from reality. There are rules in hell just as there are in life." Sere had always suspect that Professor Yates saw himself as some sort of all-knowing unseen god. The older he got, the less he tried to hide it.

"We're not talking about a run-of-the-mill doppelgänger. If we were, at this point, I'd consider walking up to his real and thrusting my knife between his ribs. The death of one person to stop the creation of a devil would be worth it. But that wouldn't work in Andy's case, would it?" she asked in as judgmental a tone as she could muster.

"No." The professor opened his battered laptop. "After what happened with Thomas, I built a safeguard into Andy. He isn't reliant on his real. Basically, he's on a projection loop. That's why he never ages. If you had killed him like you did Thomas, his consciousness wouldn't transfer to his real. He resets every forty days, which also wipes his memories clean."

"Well, I'm betting he's figured out a way of retaining what he knows. Marjory Laroque has someone in hell maintaining her power bridge to life. All those lost souls that were supposed to head to Guinee are trapped in hell.

They're the basis of the paranormal link. She's brought over a specific doppelgänger—one from her family—and she intends on infusing it with the soul of the real. First, however, she needs someone in hell to make sure her little toy's cord stays plugged in. If it's not Andy, who else could it be?"

The professor leaned back in his creaky office chair. "Your logic is sound. On my own, I couldn't have freed you from hell. It took you and Sanguine working from that side to open the door. Every energy connection between each person and their doppelgänger passes through this equipment." The screen on his laptop displayed an image of his lab in hell. "Andrew, are you there, my boy?"

"Yes, Professor." The snarky shit's face filled the screen. "What test do you want run today?"

Sere watched intently to see if he showed any hint of recognition. "Do you know who I am?" *You little doppelfucker,* she wanted to add.

"Of course. You're Sere Mal-Laurette. It's nice to finally meet you."

Sere glared at the professor. "This doesn't mean anything."

He didn't respond to her. "Andrew, please have a seat and put your hands on the computer pads."

The teenager did as instructed but with a slight hesitation. "Am I in trouble?"

"Not at all. I just need to run a quick diagnostic test. This won't hurt a bit."

"He's going to bolt," Bart whispered to Sere.

As predicted, when the professor looked down at his

keyboard and started the procedure, Andy sprang from the chair and raced for the door.

"Shit!" Sere yelled. "Can't you zap him or something?"

The professor switched the screen from camera view to external map. "I was going to perform a hard reboot, but that boy is a wily one. I did get just enough data from the connection to show he's been manipulating the resets. Looks like you were right."

"Fat lot of good that does me now."

The old man dialed in a tracker program that kept a red target painted on the running boy. "He won't be returning to my lab. That should at least make your metaphorical power plug vulnerable."

She tried to calm her anger. "He knows too much. I can't let him run around free in hell. He'll just head straight to Marjory Laroque with everything he knows. They have to have some way of communicating. How do we kill the little fucker?"

The man continued staring at the computer as if unable to comprehend how wrong he'd been to trust his own creation. "I'm afraid it will have to be done in hell. He has no connection to life."

"And he's not likely to make the jump across dimensions again." Sere grabbed Bart's hand. "Come on. I'm afraid we can't wait around for Kendell to make a diplomatic approach to Dooly Buell. Looks like I'm going to need Doodlebug a lot sooner than I'd hoped." She turned back to the professor. "Joe worked up two helmets that allowed us to communicate while on the road. If I get one to you, do you think you could use the technology to rig up a way for me to talk to the doppelgänger once she's back in hell?"

"I'm sure I can." For the first time that Sere could remember, the old man looked genuinely sorry.

WHEN THEY RETURNED to the Scratchy Dog, Sere saw a scrawny young woman sitting with Kendell at the bar. A large half-eaten pizza loaded with every type of meat Sere could imagine took up the width of the counter. From the lightly used napkins in Myles and Kendell's hands, it was clear they'd only taken token slices while the girl was devouring as much of the pizza as she could shove into her mouth.

Kendell slid off the stool. "This is Dooly Buell. As I said earlier this morning, she wasn't hard to locate. We were just starting our conversation."

"Can I get a beer?" Dooly said with her mouth full.

Though the girl was clearly underage, Sere doubted it would be her first beer—probably not even her first beer of the day. She nodded at Myles. "You can consider it one for me if it eases your bartender sense of honor." She took the seat Kendell had vacated. "I need your help."

The girl looked up from her slice of pizza and turned slightly away with intense distrust in her eyes as if Sere were trying to steal her food. "You're not some pervert, are you?"

Sere wondered how similar the girl's life on the streets had been to her doppelgänger's time in hell. "There's nothing sexual in my request. We're not going to hurt you." She wished she would be able to give the same assurance to her double. "Really, all you'll need to do is wear an ACE bandage for a while."

"What's in it for me?"

"How about we don't kill you," Bart blurted out before turning to Sere. "I'm sorry, but the fact that this girl's double killed Joe is making it hard to just stand here as if you're talking to some lost child."

"Oh yeah?" The girl sprang off the chair like a cat who'd been squirted with a water bottle. "I'd like to see you try. Big brute—think you can bully anyone smaller than you."

"Okay, that's enough." Kendell stepped in front of the fireball of a girl.

Sere put her hand on Bart's bulging bicep. "We need her."

Dooly picked up another slice of pizza but never took her eyes off of Bart. "Who's this Joe person, anyway? One of your *lovers*?"

Bart took a couple of controlled breaths before turning to Sere. "And I thought you were a handful. I'm going to step outside for a minute."

"What did he mean by my *double*?" the girl asked once Bart was safely outside.

Sere eyed the bottle of Jameson behind the bar. If she was going to earn the girl's trust, she would have to reveal more than she found comfortable. She gave Myles a quick glance, and he took the hint, grabbing a shot glass and the bottle.

"You wouldn't believe me if I told you," Sere said.

Dooly remained standing as if challenging Sere to say the wrong thing. "Try me." The girl's attitude hadn't diminished with Bart out of the room.

Sere downed the shot. "Fine. I come from hell. Not some cutesy town that thought the name would be funny—I mean the actual hell. My father was the devil. Every person you know in New Orleans has a double down in that dimension. Some of those doppelgängers, like yours, have broken free. How's my story hitting you so far?"

Doodlebug shrugged. "I've heard better bullshit, but I like your conviction."

"Your double killed a friend of ours—Joe. So we're all just a little on edge around you." Sere pulled her knife from her boot and set it on the bar. "Like Bart, I'd just as soon slice your throat to see what happens to your double as ask for your help. But we all need your double to return to hell for a mission, and that means we need you."

"Lost me," the girl announced as she grabbed the beer from the bar as if she were about to leave.

"I want your double to kill someone for me."

Dooly finally sat back down on the stool. "Now you've got my attention."

Sere reached under her hair to her shoulders, pulled the two katana swords from her back, and set them on the bar next to her knife. "More specifically, I want her to behead the little twerp."

Dooly Buell's eyes remained fixed on the gleaming blades. "What do you need me for?" The question was less belligerent and more curious than her previous inquires.

"Your double will do all the dangerous work, but I need

to convince her that she can return to our dimension once she's done. That's where the bandage comes in. Connecting you two will provide her a lifeline, literally. You should know, though, if she gets into trouble, she might draw on your energy. We'll keep you safe until she returns so if anything goes wrong we can disconnect you."

The girl recovered her composure and took another drink of her beer. "I still haven't heard what I get out of it."

"What do you want?" Negotiating wasn't something Sere wanted to drag out.

"Give me one of those swords, and show me how to use it."

Sere had to respect the practicality of the request. A girl living on the streets could use some self-protection. "Sounds fair. The other one is headed to hell with your double for the decapitation. After your double does her job, I'll let you have one and teach you both to use them."

"And I want to meet her."

"Out of the question," Kendell said. "There are paranormal forces you can't understand. It's too dangerous."

Dooly ran her hand along the edge of the sword. She pulled her fingers away and stared at the blood trickling from the cuts. "So you'll let me drink and give me a lethal weapon, but meeting my twin is off-limits? You people have some fucked-up ideas about what's dangerous."

Sere leaned her arm against the bar. "I haven't even met the woman who supplies *my* body image."

"Wait," the girl said. "You're saying you're one of these body doubles?"

"We're called doppelgängers. And yes, I am one."

"It's a little more complicated than that," Kendell said.

"Prove it." Dooly pushed the sword toward Sere.

"Fine." Sere picked up the blade and made a deep three-inch-long cut in her forearm.

"Jesus! I didn't mean for you to cut your fucking arm off. Are you crazy?" The girl edged away from Sere on the barstool.

Sere let the cut bleed to prove that she hadn't pulled a fast one. She had to demand that Dooly stay focused on the wound. "Look." Sere pulled the sides of the cut open for the girl's inspection. "Touch it if you want."

"Why would I? So you cut yourself. That doesn't prove jack shit."

Sere let go of the wound. The flesh snapped back together like it was made of Velcro. She then grabbed a napkin from the bar and wiped away the blood. The freshly healed arm didn't even have a pink line where the cut had been. "How about now?"

Dooly poked at the nonexistent wound with her dirty grease-covered fingers.

Thank God I heal up fast and am not susceptible to germs, Sere thought.

"And my double can heal like that too?" the girl asked.

"She can with your help. A simple cut like this one, and you wouldn't even notice her use your energy. If my enemy were to cut off one of her arms or stab her in a vital organ, you might feel a little woozy while wearing the bandage. That's about it. If all goes well, we'll only need you for a few days. Right now, I just need to be able to tell your double that you're on board."

Dooly grabbed the last piece of pizza. "You're a fucked-up chick, and I dig that." She aimed the slice at Kendell and Myles. "Word on the street is these two can be trusted. That monster asshole outside, however, better keep his grubby paws off me."

Sere could only imagine the hassles the girl must have endured as a teenager living on the streets. "You don't have to worry about him."

"Says you." The girl drained the last of the beer from the glass. "So I get two days of pampering in a nice hotel room, including food and beverages. You give me one of those swords and teach me to use it. And all I have to do is wear a bandage while you run your little make-believe computer game?" She shrugged as if she were considering the offer. "I guess we can give it a try. Anyone tries anything funny, though, and I'm out of there. I do have friends who will be checking on me."

Sere didn't doubt Dooly's support network for a minute. She picked up her knife. "I'll get you what you want. Just don't make me regret not killing you."

17

*S*ere tossed a sword and headband on the grass at Doodlebug's feet. The day had already been interminably long. First there was the trip back to the professor's lab with the helmet and Dooly, then they had to wait until he had whipped up the paranormal connection. Then she and Bart had spent a couple of hours getting out to Joe's half-sunken school-bus cache to retrieve his speedboat. Motoring out to Sanguine's old cabin in the swamp should have been restful, but all Sere had wanted to do was pull the boat onto some hidden island so she could explore more sexual positions with Bart. By the time they made it out to Sanguine's island, Sere was in no mood for the demon version of Dooly's snarky attitude.

The doppelgirl touched the hilt of the sword with her toe. "You're going to let me defend myself before killing me? Living in this world has made you soft."

Sere warmed up by twirling her matching sword like it

was a baseball bat and she was on deck. "I need to see if you're truly skilled or if killing Joe was a fluke." She couldn't believe that Joe would have been duped by someone who didn't know what they were doing, but he would have been the first to tell her that lucky amateurs were sometimes more dangerous than the best-trained assassins.

Doodlebug reached down for the blade without breaking eye contact with Sere. "And what about your friend in the trees, holding the shotgun?"

"I don't intend on losing my head. He's my fail-safe in case something unfortunate happens. Show me what you've got without killing me, and we'll talk. Now put on the headband."

The girl aimed the blade at Sere. "Fuck you. You put it on."

Sere could tell this was going to be a long night. "Without you wearing one, it wouldn't work on me. Now, put the damn thing on like a good little doppelgirl. We've got a lot of work ahead of us."

Doodlebug kept her sword pointed at Sere and reached down for the sweatband. "This thing looks like part of a fucking '80s Halloween costume. What's it supposed to do —zap me if I don't behave?"

Sere pulled her hair away from her head to show the earpiece. "Testing your fighting skills is only part of the experiment. If this technology works, it could keep you from disintegrating. Now, stop delaying the inevitable."

The girl dropped the tip of the sword to her feet as if she were thinking up another question. When Sere lowered hers in exasperation, however, Doodlebug took a step forward and sliced through the air with the blade as if swinging a tennis racket.

Sere saw the feint coming a mile away. By tilting her blade up at an angle over her head she deflected the attack without turning away from the demon. Doodlebug had put so much of her small body behind the swing that she'd left her stomach undefended as her blade sailed over Sere's head. Sere swung her sword toward the girl's torso. Like Joe during training, she didn't show any mercy. She drew the blade deep into the girl's flesh, exposing ribs and organs.

Doodlebug fell to the ground. "So you *are* going to kill me. Just get it over with."

"Shut up," Sere said. Sympathy hadn't been a part of her combat training. "Get off the ground and face me. First rule of fighting: don't feel sorry for yourself."

"Fuck you." The demon girl rolled to her back and looked like she was about to cry.

Was I ever this much of a drama queen? Sere wondered. "Get up right now. You don't want to get dirt in your wound, or it won't heal correctly. Second rule: keep your wounds clean."

Doodlebug held her arm across a cut that would have killed a normal person and struggled to stay out of the dirt. "You fucking cut the muscles."

"This is the last time I'm saying this. Get up!" Sere began to understand Joe's impatience during her early training sessions with him. "If that attack is the best you've got, you're no use to me." She took her sword with both hands and raised it over her head for the decapitation.

The girl quickly doubled up over her sliced abdomen

and worked her way to her knees. By the time she struggled back to her feet, the cut was no more than a red line across her stomach. She looked at her abdomen in confusion. "How?"

"I'm not here to explain things to you." Sere brought her blade back to the attack position. "This is a test, and you're failing."

Doodlebug raised her sword with one hand on the handle and the other on the blade as though she'd watched too many martial-arts movies. "Fine, bitch. Let's do this."

Sere knew better than to take the girl for granted. She tried an over-the-shoulder attack that the girl easily parried. Unlike Doodlebug's initial attack, however, Sere kept her weight centered, allowing her to be set for the countermove. The girl tried the same response that Sere had used but found Sere's sword at the ready.

"Copying my strategies is fine for training, but I hope you'll be more imaginative than just parroting what I do. Show me you've got something more in that head of yours than simply your doppelgänger instincts."

The swords started flying and crashing like a samurai battle to the death. What the girl lacked in training, she compensated for with creativity and cunning. After half an hour of swinging the blade, Doodlebug dropped her sword and fell to her knees. "I can't go on." She struggled to catch her breath enough to form the words. "Just kill me if you're going to do it. Why do you have to torture me?"

Her pleading made Sere consider the offer. She swung her sword as if getting ready to fulfill Doodlebug's fear. "Rule number three: you are *not* tired. Your body is a machine. So long as there's energy to run it, you can go on indefinitely. *Tired* is for humans. Now, pick up that sword. Weapons aren't to be discarded until you're dead. And don't ever ignore rule number one. Feeling sorry for yourself will only piss me off." She could hear Joe telling a young Sere exactly the same thing.

The battle raged uninterrupted for three more hours. For each slice to the shoulder or leg that Doodlebug landed, Sere cut the girl deep to the stomach or chest. Sere's cuts healed nearly as fast as the blades clashed. The girl wasn't as fortunate. From the professor's lab, Sere was getting updates on Dooly's ability to supply Doodlebug with healing energy. Both real and doppelgänger were struggling with their new connection. But at least Joe's communication wavelength worked as intended.

Finally, Bart fired the shotgun into the air. "That's enough, Sere. You're just showing off, and it's getting boring."

Sere held her blade out toward Doodlebug in case the girl had any bright ideas of fighting during the imposed truce. "Not bad. Not great but good enough to decapitate the demon I'm sending you after." She didn't feel tired. Instead, the blood that pumped through her oxygen-deprived muscles powered her up like jet fuel. She felt ready to take on all of hell's demons single-handed.

"So I win your approval?" Doodlebug had drool running down her chin. Her eyes were demon red, but she'd never turned into the unrestrained animal combatant that Sere had encountered with other doppelgängers.

"Rule number four: you don't need and will never get my

approval. Learn to be like that sword—the weapon proves its worth but doesn't expect recognition. However, you have won the position of my champion in hell. I'm sending you back to kill someone for me. Consider it payment for having murdered Joe: a life for a life."

The girl used her torn army shirt to wipe the small amount of Sere's blood off her sword. "Then we'll be square?"

"Not even close," Sere said. "But do this for me, and I'll let you return to this dimension, where I can keep an eye on you. How did you learn to fight, anyway? Your real has a lot of spunk, but she doesn't seem capable of defending herself from a bunny rabbit."

Doodlebug straightened up and held her sword tip down like a conquering hero. "I remember being like that girl. Then I watched you decapitate that harvester in hell. Seeing you fight changed my life. I'd never heard of anyone, especially a woman, going up against one of those fiends and surviving. I have a really good memory, so I started copying every move you made. There aren't many fight instructors in hell, but I found one willing to train me." She lifted the blade and turned it in the late-morning light. "This was my first time using a sword, though. I liked it. So I'll go back to hell for you. I just want your assurance that I can come back here."

"I just said you could, didn't I?"

"*When I'm ready.* There are a couple of harvesters I'd like to deal with while I'm there. If you're not going to be hell's avenging superhero, I'd like the job—even if it's only temporary."

"I'll do you one better. Be my representative in hell, and I'll teach your real how to fight. Her muscle skills will transfer to you, and you can observe the training over that headband. There's only one condition. When you return to life, you and your real can never meet. You'll have to build your life on the Northshore."

"I can live with that," Doodlebug said. "I don't think I could face the real version of New Orleans anyway. I'd see harvesters around every corner."

"Wonderful," Sere said without enthusiasm. Negotiating with a demon who should have been happy just to be able to keep her head was nearly as distasteful as agreeing to her real's terms. Sere turned away from Doodlebug and walked to the water's edge. "Lefty. Here, boy."

The thirty-foot gator swam out of the reeds, wearing a crown of wildflowers between his yellow-green eyes.

Sere put her hands on her hips. "What the fuck, dude?"

"We were bored waiting for you," Doodlebug said from the clearing.

"Well, I hope you two enjoyed your vacation," Sere said to the gator. "It's time to get back to work. The only way to get Doodlebug back to hell without being detected by our enemies is for you to swim her through the hell mouth. Bart and I will follow along in the boat as far as the crystal-blue water. Don't dally once you're there. Drop her off, and get that tail back as soon as possible. I don't have time for your shenanigans."

"Do you think she can do it?" Dooly stuck so close to Sere's side in the professor's laboratory that Sere began to understand the concept of an annoying little sister.

Sere was down to her last nerve. It had taken all afternoon to ride out to the swamp with Bart and then boat out to the cabin. Her fight with Doodlebug had taken the better part of the night. Then there was the swamp tour to make sure Doodlebug and Lefty made the journey to hell and the subsequent wait for Lefty's return. By the time Sere and Bart returned to New Orleans, it was once again daylight. At least Doodlebug had likewise found her way to hell's version of the city.

"She'll do it or die trying. If she can't even track down and kill a doppelshit lab geek, she won't stand a chance against the harvesters."

"I heard that," Doodlebug said through Sere's earpiece.

"I think I've got it," Polly yelled from the office hallway. "Try it now, Professor."

The wall screen that had been displaying a map with Andy's location as a red dot transformed into a view of the city tormented by the never-ending hurricane-driven rain.

"Okay," Sere said. "We can see what you're seeing."

"How does that do me one fucking bit of good?" Doodlebug demanded over the transmission.

"It probably doesn't," Sere conceded. "But it is more entertaining."

"Fuck you." The girl hunkered down along the iron fence of Jackson Square and crept toward Saint Louis Cathedral. "Now, which way did he go?"

Sere checked the smaller screen that still tracked Andy's

location. "He's still trying to get to the bank. The professor has been manipulating the streets into a maze, so that nerdy demon has been going around in circles. The little twerp is getting pretty frustrated. Just watch out for harvesters."

Doodlebug held the sword, edge first, toward her eyes as if she wanted to slice Sere on the other end of the transmission. "You've got the nerve to tell me about harvesters? Jesus, woman. You spend a few hours here and think you know all about life in this enhanced hell."

"Do you really want to have a debate right now?" Sere asked.

"You started it," the girl grumbled. She slunk back down and ran through the rain to the roofline that covered the sidewalk. "Tell that professor of yours that I'm making a left onto Chartres Street. I don't want him putting me back on Decatur again. I'm trying to get ahead of Andy, not follow the bastard."

"He *can* hear you." To keep from overly distracting Doodlebug, only Sere could talk to her even though everyone in the lab was eavesdropping on the conversation. Sere, however, also had her matching paranormal headband, allowing her to hear the girl's thoughts. *The three of us look like a cheesy girl band from the 1980s.*

You're telling me, Doodlebug responded.

Dooly Buell looked around the room with wide eyes as if certain she was losing her mind.

"I can't just change one intersection," the professor said. "Moving things around in hell is like turning a Rubik's Cube. I'm sorry if keeping Andy from getting to the bank is inconveniencing Doodlebug. I can't do much about that."

The old man kept banging out computer code through his complaints.

"He's doing his best," Sere relayed to Doodlebug.

"Tell her to make a right at the next intersection," the professor called out from behind his computer. "And tell her not to look at the damn street signs. Andy will be coming at her from a block away. That should give her time to set up her ambush."

Sere gave her warrior the message. "He'll be armed— probably with a gun."

"What would a bullet do to me?"

"I don't know," Sere said. "But it'd be best if we didn't find out. The twerp might not be much good at fighting, but coming up with dastardly doppelgänger ordnance seems to be his forte."

"Cut off his head. Don't get shot. Got it." Doodlebug ducked into a doorway to wait for her prey.

Unfortunately, she wasn't the only one on the hunt. The door she leaned against swung open, and a bony hand yanked her by the shoulder into the dark entry. "Skilled little minx, aren't you? I'll find plenty of buyers for those arms and legs." The harvester sliced at her with a reaping hook. The blade cut her to the bone but didn't cleave her arm from her body.

"Spin to your left while the blade is still stuck in you," Sere instructed. "You're going to wrench it out of his hand."

Next to Sere, Dooly Buell sagged to the floor, though Sere couldn't tell if it was from the energy exchange or the impossibility of what the waif was witnessing. Myles was on his knees next to Dooly before she completely passed out. "Hang in there, girl."

Sere didn't have time for the theatrics. "Don't draw on your real until the knife is out of your arm. Remember, no foreign matter, or the wound won't heal."

Doodlebug grabbed the sickle and spun so hard she flipped the harvester over her back. "Now what?"

"Take the damn knife out of your arm, and lob off the bastard's head." Sere tried not to yell, but stating the obvious during a fight had a way of bringing out the same intensity Joe had shown during training.

With the curved blade finally dislodged, Doodlebug swung the back side of the weapon at the harvester's throat. Though it crushed a vertebra, the head remained attached.

"Use the goddamned sword!"

The girl was already reaching for the handle. "Don't yell at me." With a swing of her good arm, she decapitated the harvester like it was a rag doll.

"Andy's almost at the door," the professor announced from behind his computer screen.

"Get moving, girl," Sere said. "This may be your only chance at attack before Andy figures out your play."

With the sickle in one hand and the sword in the other, Doodlebug ran to the open door. She swung the long straight blade backhanded through the opening. It lodged hard into flesh.

When she stepped out of the entryway, Andy lifted his gun at her chest. "Don't make me kill you." His voice trembled nearly as badly as the hand holding his weapon.

Blood was squirting so hard from between his arms that it was hard to tell the pelting rain from the geyser of red.

Acting more on instinct than training, Doodlebug swung the sickle up and cut his hand from his arm. The gun went skidding into the street and disappeared into a storm drain. A rat the size of a milk crate rushed out from the shadows and ran off with the twerp's hand. "Sere was right. You're nothing more than bird shit on the devil's waistcoat."

The computer display transitioned from the blues and grays of the storm to shades of demonic red. "Maintain control, Doodlebug. All you have to do now is cut off his head," Sere said.

But the girl had gone full demon. Like the whirling blades of a Cuisinart, she sliced and diced the lab geek until he was completely unrecognizable as anything more than a pulpy red mess. Sere wasn't sure if the colors she was seeing on the monitor were from the girl's continued demonic state or the blood that covered every square inch of the building's entrance.

SERE WAITED until the girl finally lowered her blades. "Feel better?"

"Invigorated," Doodlebug said between breaths. "I now understand rule number three. I could fight like this for days. What's next?"

So far, the experiment of sending Doodlebug into hell had exceeded Sere's expectations, but killing Andy wouldn't stop Marjory Laroque. They needed a better look behind the paranormal scene to figure out what their adversary was up to. "Find the hell version of the professor's laboratory. We need to see how close they've come to raising a devil."

Through the darkness, Doodlebug dodged demons, downpours, and distorted intersections to get from the Quarter to the professor's hell-based laboratory. She swung both sword and sickle with zeal at each potential threat. Every burst of Doodlebug's adrenaline over the paranormal headband made Sere wish she were fighting alongside the girl.

"She's enjoying this new power far too much," Polly said. "We may have just created another monster."

"She's doing what she needs to do to survive." Sere would never forgive the doppelbitch for killing Joe, but seeing hell through the girl's eyes made violence seem as necessary and normal as strong coffee to someone working the night shift.

Doodlebug pressed her back to the wall next to the broken-glass door. "Okay. I'm here. Please tell me there isn't some doppelgänger professor on the other side of this door."

The diorama that displayed hell and its inhabitants had an annoying way of being inaccurate. Lightning strikes that were as much bursts of paranormal energy as the release of cloud friction made entire city blocks of doppelgängers momentarily invisible to the computer's sensors.

"Assuming the professor's safeguards are working correctly, there shouldn't be anyone inside," Sere said.

Professor Yates hooked an alligator clip to Dooly Buell's

headband. The attached wire connected to his computer. "She can enter now."

Sere noticed a blue aura form around Doodlebug. "Go for it."

Doodlebug held both her weapons to her chest as she rolled her body through the door. "You're sure there's no one here?"

Sere wasn't sure of anything. "Stay on guard. That little twerp was in charge of the lab for far too long. It wouldn't surprise me if he figured out a way to bypass the professor's security."

The girl ducked below the worktable. "Well, something's not right. I can hear screaming, but it's muffled, like it's in the next room."

"Be careful, Doodlebug," Sere said.

"Careful, schmareful," the girl muttered as she used her sword to prod everything she saw.

Before Sere could chastise the girl, Polly snickered. "I swear, she sounds exactly like you at that age. Joe was the only one who could get you to listen to reason."

"This isn't really the time for reminiscing." Sere inspected the diorama again. "I'm not seeing anyone in there other than you."

"Fuck." Doodlebug sprang out from under the table as if she were about to slice off someone's head. "The voices aren't from this dimension. Look." She pointed her sword at the screens along the wall of the professor's offices.

What the girl saw had to be transmitted between dimensions to Dooly Buell then downloaded into the professor's bank of computers to be translated into what humans could see. As such, it took everyone in the room a moment to understand the scribbles that waved in front of the girl's eyes.

"Good lord," Sere said as her doppelgänger eyes picked out the tortured souls before the rest of the people in the room had a chance to see what was happening. "It's every person the demons killed in this dimension. They're being held captive in the computer's software."

"We expected that," Professor Yates said. "Their suffering is what our enemies are using to hold open the rift between dimensions."

"Pull the fucking plug," Sere said.

"No." The professor got up from his Barcalounger. "Those souls are like water in a hose. We're holding one end of it with our equipment in hell, and Marjory is holding the other somewhere in the bank. If you disconnect the souls, either we'll be handing them over to her, or those spirits will evaporate into hell's dimension. They'll be stuck there forever as tortured ghosts. To save them, we either need to connect to them in this reality or find a way to collect them in hell. Ultimately, we need to bring them to this side so the loas of the dead can escort them to Guinee and, finally, the *deep waters*, where they belong. I can see the problem, but it'll take some work to figure out how to tie in the differing dimensions."

"And we'll need the loas ready and waiting," Kendell said.

"Fuck!" Sere really wished she could decapitate a demon to ease her frustration.

Doodlebug held out her blades as if she expected

someone to walk in on her. "That's all very nice, but can we get back to what I'm supposed to be doing here?"

Sere tried directing the girl's eyes to the computer icons, but Doodlebug was more fascinated with the trapped souls.

"Find me the information on those that escaped with you," Sere said.

Doodlebug looked down at the aged desktop computer and opened the most recent file. The computer screen filled with doppelgänger mug shots. "I never knew any of their identities," Doodlebug said. "We got our instructions through telepathic communication. Now that I've heard Andy's voice, I recognized it as the one directing the action."

"I don't care," Sere said. "Find me the damn asshole that I met out in the swamp."

Bart pointed at one of the pictures. "That's the guy. I never forget the face of someone I've killed, even if that person isn't real."

Sere leaned in close. Another face next to the first was so similar they could have been brothers separated by only a handful of years. "Yep, this is the one." She read off the name of the demon they'd killed. "Creed Laroque. Based on him being in charge of the demons out in the swamp, I'll bet he was as close as they could come to someone who understood the bayou. Doodlebug, I've got a mission for you. Find this asshole, and cut off his head. Without Andy at the controls, Creedy Boy won't be able to retain the memories he apparently cherishes so much. Make him suffer."

"Gladly." The girl pointed at the neighboring picture. "What about his cousin?"

"Devlin Laroque," Sere read out loud. "He's still in our dimension."

"Don't let her leave yet." Kendell bit her lip and stared at the tabletop display of hell. "Doodlebug might be more useful right where she is. If our diorama is this glitchy, Marjory might not know Andy's been decapitated. Whatever she's using to see hell couldn't be better than what we have right here." She turned to the professor. "Your hell-based lab is off-limits to any doppelgänger you don't let in, so Marjory isn't going to be able to find out who's working for her from the other side. Could we make it look like Doodlebug is actually Andy?"

The professor waved his pipe at the screen. "Ask the girl how well she understands computers."

"Apparently about as well as you people understand hell," Doodlebug replied.

Polly pressed the transmit button on the nickel-plated microphone from the office's old public-address system. "If you're going to copy Andy's actions, we'll need to know what he's been up to. You need to find the professor's laptop. It will probably be gathering dust in some dark corner of the lab. We can work over that computer without anyone listening in." The words, transmitted to hell then back to the professor's equipment in life, sounded like the voice of God.

"I'm not some fucking lab geek," Doodlebug yelled. "I only agreed to come back to hell to kill whoever Sere instructs me to and the harvesters I hate. Working these damn computers wasn't part of the arrangement."

"Have her pull up all twelve files on the screen," the

professor said. "They'll just look like gibberish, but I can copy them to my computer. I can at least figure out who stayed among the living and if any of them have been infected with a human soul."

Polly grasped the side of the desk with one hand and the microphone with the other. "One person at a time. Doodlebug, you're going to have to stay in the office until Sere can confront Marjory. If our enemy realizes you haven't regenerated in hell, they'll know we're messing with their bridge. You going on a killing spree will only show our hand. So long as you're stuck there, you might as well be of some use. If I teach both you and Dooly at the same time about hell's software, maybe one of you will learn something. But even if you don't, we need to fool Marjory for as long as possible."

SERE HAD NEVER CARED much for science. Staring at the pile of printouts made her head hurt. "What does all this stuff mean? Have they transferred a human consciousness into their pet doppelpuppet or not?" Though she and Bart had speculated on Marjory not yet completing her monster, Sere really needed to know what she was up against before doing battle.

The professor stood up from the table and lifted his empty pipe from the square green-glass ashtray. "I don't believe so." He packed the bowl with tobacco in his infuriatingly slow manner. "As you know, time in hell doesn't move. Other than when your father was in charge, we've been able to hold the realm to midnight."

Sere stared at the acoustical-tile covered ceiling. "*Please don't tell me what I already know.*"

He held a match to the pipe and took three agonizingly slow draws before answering. "From the computer notes, Andy believed the time in hell needed to correspond to the time in life. So midnight is when they'll be conducting their experiments. Based on Fisher's information, they've only had the doppelgänger in their lab for two days. They aren't going to kill their real until they're positive they can transfer the consciousness to the new body."

Sere turned to Polly. "Can you please get him to skip to the point?"

Polly pointed at the computer's time log. "To transfer the soul, it will have to pass from life to hell and then back out to the doppelgänger body in life on the bridge they created. If they'd made the transfer of spirit to doppelgänger, there would have been a burst of energy at that time, and there wasn't. Marjory will be relying on Andy to make sure the transfer works from hell's side of the experiment."

"Now that Andy is dust, is there any way we can prevent the transfer of soul to doppelgänger?" Bart asked.

The professor pointed the stem of his pipe at the screen. "Andy had a long time to set up the equipment. He probably has everything they need already programmed in."

Polly checked the old-fashioned clock left over from when the office had handled shipments from the wharf. "If we assume they're going to try tonight, that only leaves six hours for me to train Doodlebug. That's not enough time to change the program."

The professor took a draw on his pipe and let out a cloud of blue smoke. "If we could get a look at the transfer while it's happening—not just from the software's perspective but also the actual act—we'd have a much better idea of what Marjory is up to. I doubt this will be the only time she tries to create an immortal."

Sere held Bart's hand. "That gives us six hours to figure out how to break into the bank's basement." She turned to Kendell. "Contact Fisher and have him meet us at the bar with whatever information he has on the bank's layout. Polly and the professor already have enough work piled up in this office."

"One other thing," the professor said between bursts of blue smoke from his pipe. "Once they make the transfer, simply cutting off the head of the devil might not end his existence, as both real and demon will coexist inside the doppelgänger body. And filling him full of paranormal shotgun pellets won't sever the connection as the two will be fused into one."

"So he'll no longer need the connection to hell?" Sere asked. Such a possibility would put him well beyond her grasp.

"More like he had a backup battery," Professor Yates said. "He'll still need the connection, but he'll be able to survive for stints without it. The longer he goes without a recharge, the weaker he'll become. That's why cutting off his head won't necessarily end him. If it's off his neck long enough, however, he'll run out of juice. Fighting him isn't going to be as straightforward as destroying a demon."

"Any idea how long I'd need to keep him unplugged?"

The professor shrugged as if the question was nothing more than a theoretical contemplation. "We're beyond my science at this point."

She'd already seen the result of pulling one side off of the battery with Thomas. *Back to the fucking chalkboard again?* Sere patted Bart on the butt close to the gun he kept lodged in the back of his pants. "I figured as much. That's why I've got my contingency plan right here."

isher unrolled a large blueprint of the bank's basement across the bar at the Scratchy Dog. "Here are the results of my inquiries."

Myles pulled out some glass beer steins and used them to weigh down the corners of the paper. "You found all that information and had a blueprint created in *thirty-six* hours? Do you have any idea how long it took us to get an architect to even listen to our ideas regarding this bar's remodel?"

Fisher's eyes twinkled as he winked at Myles. "I've done a lot of people's taxes and gotten more than a few folks out of some financial trouble. When I dial the phone, people pick up."

Myles shook his head as he inspected the complexity of the document. "Next time I need anything done in this city, I'm calling you."

Sere leaned over the white lines on blue paper. "What am I looking at?"

Fisher pulled out his trusty pen and used it as a pointer. "First thing to notice is that there's only one door. This basement was built as a bunker."

"Great," Bart said with sarcasm in his voice. "One way in and undoubtedly under heavy guard."

Fisher smiled up at Bart as if he had cards in his hand that he was just dying to play. "Next thing is the size of the walls: thirty inches of reinforced concrete. They weren't messing around."

"Why don't you skip to the good news?" Sere asked.

Fisher straightened up and slid the page half off the bar until one wall of the diagram was centered on the counter. He then pulled out a yellowed piece of paper that looked like a treasure map and laid it next to the wall on the blueprint. "Fine, but you're ruining part of the fun. After the War Between the States, Baron Malveaux made some modifications to the old bank—most notably, this access tunnel. It runs from the basement under Conti Street all the way to Basin Street. After the war, the South experienced a surge of puritanical respectability that made the Baron's activities even less popular than they'd been before. Using this passage, he could get from the bank to his brothels without being seen in public. As he got older and more concerned with power than sex, he had the passage bricked in. The bombing of the old bank was mostly designed to destroy the Baron's hidden office, not collapse the entire structure. When they poured the new basement walls alongside the existing crumbling ones, no one bothered doing an excavation of what was around the bank."

"I remember," Kendell said. "The city kept promoting

how fast the bank was being rebuilt as a way of showing what was possible in New Orleans."

"What they didn't say," Fisher continued, "was that corners were cut. Based on what was paid to the demolition crew, the remaining basement walls had been cleaned up but not removed. Marjory Laroque was busy figuring out how to retain customers and power. She wasn't interested in concrete pours." Fisher drew a dotted line on the blueprint corresponding to the tunnel on the yellowed piece of paper. "This section right here is little more than sand and rebar covered by a thin layer of plaster finish. The old shaft didn't have the same soil makeup as the rest of the ground, making the concrete mixture unstable. From the information my source provided, it never did set correctly."

"So how do we get into this hidden tunnel?" Bart asked.

Fisher scribbled a Conti Street address on a napkin. "This building is in the midst of a renovation. The contractor is a client of mine. He'll get you in and supply you with what you need, no questions asked. His crew pulls out at nine, and you'll want to be there shortly after they leave. That'll only give you three hours to get through the tunnels and dig a hole through the concrete wall."

Sere put her hand on the CPA's back. "You've really earned your associate-superhero stripes this week."

SERE CHECKED to make sure the handle of her katana sword was well hidden behind her hair. Instinctively, she felt for the holstered shotgun that wasn't there. "I hate going up against demons without being fully armed."

"You've got me and my gun." Bart pulled the sheet of plywood away from the doorframe of the gutted three-story building. "Man, if these walls could talk."

Sere glared at him with all of her demonic presence. "It's their talking that created the doppelgängers in the first place, or didn't you even listen to my story?"

A single lit bulb hanging from the roughhewn rafter illuminated his toothy grin. "I meant it as a joke."

She squeezed into the work space. Sawdust, decaying brick mortar, and history hung thick in the air. "I'm not sure this is the best time for humor."

"I disagree. Right before a big battle, my troops were always at their funniest."

She ducked below some reinforcing beams. "So you were in charge of your platoon? Interesting. Someday, you're going to have to give me your story the way I confided in you. Or is your history *classified*?"

"This will have to be a conversation for later." He swung his leg over the edge of an aluminum extension ladder that descended into what looked like the bowels of the earth. "I think I hear our contact banging around down there."

"That or the devil," Sere said under her breath as she followed him down to the basement.

The bright light of a high-powered flashlight caught them before they reached the bottom. "Who sent you?"

Sere shielded her eyes from the beam. "Montgomery Fisher said you could help us."

"Come on down. Watch your step. The mud can be

slippery." The beam of light moved from Sere and Bart to a small hole lined with pipes. "We were hunting down a water leak when we stumbled across the old brick cave. Originally, I thought it had been a sewer—sure smelled bad enough to be one. You two must be loco to want to explore it, but when Mr. Fisher asks for a favor, I know better than to ask why or form suspicions. Do you want me to wait for you?"

Bart stuck his head down the shaft. "We'll be okay. Fisher said something about some demolition tools we might be able to borrow?"

"Down toward the end, just before it dumps out into the old brick tunnel. Good luck with whatever the hell it is you're doing." The man turned and scampered up the ladder without ever showing his face.

"Friendly, isn't he?" Sere asked sarcastically.

"Compartmentalization." Bart hunched over and started squirming down the hole. "Why does it feel like I'm crawling down to hell to confront the devil?"

As Sere followed him, she had the same impression. "Because we are. Though, I'd take the smell of fire and brimstone over a hundred years of built-up muck under a street in the French Quarter any day."

"Agreed. I think I'm at the end." He handed back a five-foot-long metal pick and flashlight before crawling over the edge into darkness.

She fell more than crawled out of the muddy shaft into the brick-lined tunnel. "And I thought the hole out of the basement smelled bad."

Bart explored the walls with his flashlight. "Looks like

every construction project over the last hundred years decided this was a good place to dump their trash. I'd be willing to bet the methane generated from all this crap is what prevented the concrete from curing correctly." He aimed the light far down the tunnel. "At least Fisher didn't have us start all the way at Basin Street. Let's get going."

AT THEIR DESTINATION, Sere thrust the heavy metal bar hard into the wall of muck. "I thought Fisher said this was made up of crumbling bricks."

"This is what's left of it." Bart rammed his bar in next to Sere's. "Between the city's high water table and countless sewer leaks, these buildings practically float."

Her next hit penetrated the layer of mud, brick, and rock to reveal the fine gray sand mixed with powder of the most recent addition to the foundation. "Finally."

Bart stripped off his shirt and started going at the wall like a demolition machine. Never before had Sere experienced such uncontrolled lust as she felt while watching his arms and abs—glistening with sweat—bulge and ripple as they powered the iron bar through the moist wall. His leg and butt muscles flexed so large she wondered how the skintight black jeans were able to contain them.

"I'm through." The dim light from inside the basement reflected off his glistening skin. He pulled out a chunk of blue-gray-painted plaster and tossed it at her feet like a gladiator's tribute to his queen. "The rebar is too close together for me to fit inside the basement. I should be able to lie in the hole and aim my gun. Once you're inside, you'll have to flush the human-possessed demon into my range."

She swallowed down her longing and checked her watch. "Just in time."

He moved out of the opening, dropped his five-foot iron pole, and wrapped his arms around her. "Don't go getting yourself hurt in there. Get in. Get past the two guardian demons. Flush the devil into the open so I can shoot him. And get your cute little ass back here. I don't want to tear this bank down block by block to free you, but I will if you get captured."

She didn't doubt him for a moment. "I'll be careful. I promise."

"I didn't say be careful. I said don't get hurt."

She melted against his rock-hard body and nuzzled her cheek to his bare chest. "You know me so well."

SERE STRUGGLED between the rough iron bars and quietly squirmed into the bank's basement. Evenly spaced pillars filled the huge open space like the under structure of a Roman coliseum. The light that had seemed so bright coming into the dark tunnel filtered past the columns from the far side of the room. Indistinct voices echoed off the walls. She turned back to Bart, who looked like a forlorn dog caged behind the rebar. "They're on the opposite side of the room. I'm going to sneak up behind the pillars. Maybe I can get some indication of what they're doing."

He pulled the gun out from the back of his jeans. "Sure you don't want a little added firepower?"

She checked the sword sheathed against her back. "I'd probably just ricochet the bullet and end up hitting myself. I'll be okay with this bad boy."

"Keep track of how many pillars you pass. Once you start ducking from one to the next, this room will seem like a maze." He stuck his head through the opening. "I've got a clear shot to the far wall and an angled shot past a couple of columns on either side."

"Got it." She leaned down and kissed him. "Just watch who you're shooting in the shadows."

Once Bart was well hidden in the darkness of the tunnel, Sere snuck to the first pillar. If there were guards, they were too busy watching the action to pay any attention to her supposedly secure end of the basement. She tiptoed through the shadows from column to column until she could hear what was happening.

"I didn't sign up for this." The man's voice echoed off the walls. "Take off these restraints."

Sere put her hand on the cold concrete pillar and edged her head out until she could see what was going on. Three columns down, a candelabra on an ornate gold table provided the only light in the room. Facing the table and away from Sere was a naked man with his wrists tied behind him.

A woman in a gray pants suit that matched the color of her hair paced on the far side of the table. Even approaching eighty years of age, Marjory Laroque could command a room. Other than the black walking cane she used as she strutted, she showed no signs of infirmity. "Perhaps you weren't *listening*. This is exactly what you signed up for."

"You said I would be in charge. This doesn't feel like being in charge."

The woman stood tall as if her backbone was made of iron. "I said you would have to fight for control."

The man struggled against the bindings on his wrists. "How am I supposed to fight if I'm naked with my hands tied?"

"It's not that kind of fight. How exactly did you think you were going to change bodies?" She reached her cane across the table and struck him in the chest with the end. "This body must die before you can inhabit the new one."

"I thought you were just going to hook me up like the devil's daughter does to her real."

Sere edged slightly farther out for a better look. Other than a distinctive well-formed backside, the man could have been almost anyone. From her new vantage point, she saw the iron box nestled close to a pillar beyond the table. A rapping from inside indicated it wasn't empty.

"Once we're done, you won't have to rely on the psychic connection she needs to survive. If you can't fight your own demon, you'll have no chance against her." Marjory came around the table then leaned against the edge directly in front of the man. "For this to work, your double must kill you. He'll then devour your soul."

"I thought you said I'd have a fighting chance. I'm not some goddamned sacrificial lamb."

The old woman didn't bother hiding her look of longing as she surveyed the struggling naked man. "Indeed you're not. Having the demon eat your essence is how you will be cast into hell."

The two doppelgängers stirred near the pillars on either side of him. Clearly, they expected an escape attempt. To his credit, the man stood firm. "I was to be in charge."

"And you shall be. If you're worthy. Once your soul is in hell, my army of the damned will escort you back to our realm. *That* is when you have to fight. Your doppelgänger body in that magic box will be inhabited by both you and your demon double. The one who wins the spiritual contest of wills will be the one to take charge." The clacking of her cane as she walked back to the iron vault filled the room. "Do not fail me, Devlin. Your options are: immortality and the power that I can give you, subjugation to a demon for all eternity, or having your soul cast into hell. Now do you understand what's at stake?"

"You should have told me."

With a quick flick of her fingers, the two demons rushed the naked man and took him by the arms. "The guinea pig isn't consulted regarding the scientist's test. Survive this, and we'll talk about your new role in my plan. Fail, and suffer for all eternity." She put one hand on the long handle that connected to the iron bars of the door's latches. "The moment this door opens, you two toss him in. If the demon inside escapes, kill Devlin, but do *not* eat his soul. Disobey me, and I'll kill your reals just to watch you two dissolve into nothingness."

When the door swung open, Sere crept even farther from her hiding spot. With everyone focused on the demon that lurked in the darkness of the box, she was able to sneak up to the pillar closest to the action. Devlin struggled against his two captors, but he was no match for them. They threw him into the cabinet as if tossing a garbage bag into a dumpster. When Marjory slammed the door shut, the man's screams of horror filled the basement.

The woman clicked the stem of a stopwatch and returned to the table. Without the naked man blocking Sere's view, she saw the journal that lay open under the candelabra. Marjory traced along the open page with her finger.

As a child, Sere hadn't been conscious during her transfer to Jennifer's doppelgänger. In her time inhabiting the body, she'd never encountered an inner demon. The body had been a blank slate on which Sere had scribbled her life's work. She couldn't imagine that her father—evil as he was—would have been so cruel as to toss her soul into a cage match with a demon the way Marjory just had. *Looks like you missed a page—or did you intend on inflicting your heir with a demon?*

Sere reminded herself that, according to Polly, the battery-powered body might not function without both demon and real soul. She grasped the handle of her sword. Fighting evil she understood. Paranormal science she left to Polly and the professor.

"It's time. Open the door," Marjory called to the demons. She turned away from the book and leaned back against the table.

Like Marjory, Sere stood transfixed, waiting to see what emerged. Though she lived in a doppelgänger body, there'd never been anyone like her. Thomas and Fisher were humans possessed by demons, but up until that moment, Sere was the only human *inhabiting* a demon. A part of her hoped Devlin would survive the transformation, but a stronger part prompted her to reach for the sword sheathed against her back. *Time to kill some demons and maybe even have a go at a devil.*

"You can come out now," Marjory called into the darkness of the cabinet.

"We're not alone." The voice from the shadows had the deep command of a person used to being in charge and ended in the low growl of a demon.

Marjory spun around and locked her stare on Sere. "Kill her!" she called to the two demons beside the cabinet as she pointed at Sere with her cane.

One of the demons turned to her. "But what about the power connection that keeps us alive?"

Marjory hit him so hard with her cane that Sere wondered how the black wood hadn't splintered. "You idiot." She patted the chest of the monster that emerged from the cabinet. "This is the master you serve now. He'll provide for your demonic needs."

19

Sere didn't get much of a chance to inspect her new hybrid brother. The two full-fledged demons ran at her like wild dogs in pursuit of a rabbit. Each one held knives ready to carve her up into bite-sized morsels.

She hit the floor and rolled behind the closest pillar. She lacked the time to conduct her tactical analysis, but since coordinated attacks weren't the demons' natural play, she had the edge. Without Andy at the controls, they'd be looking to their new leader for guidance, and he would still be figuring out his new reality. The lack of organization gave her an advantage but only so long as she kept one step ahead.

The two panted so hard she could hear their every move. She edged along the side of the column to keep it between her and her pursuers. When she had a clear shot at the next pillar, she bolted for it before the demons rounded the corner to see what she was up to. *One row of columns closer to*

Bart's field of fire—two more to go, and the closer I can get to the far wall, the better shot he'll have.

"Where are you going, sister?" The words from the newly formed devil echoed around the room.

She turned toward the far wall, away from the demons, so that her words would also echo and not reveal her position. "Why don't you poke your nose out and see? Or are you too chickenshit to face me yourself?"

"I think I'll let my henchdemons soften you up a bit first."

Sere listened for the two in pursuit. Their breathing grew shallow, making it impossible to detect their location. From the unified scuffing of their feet against the concrete, she knew the devil had taken charge of his minions. *You're using the two as twin puppets. It took Andy a few attempts to understand how to best use the demons as well.*

As she rushed toward the next pillar, the two demons emerged and gave chase. This time, however, she wasn't attempting to find another hiding spot. With a running handspring that momentarily set the sword on the floor, she managed to launch her body feetfirst toward the concrete column. The demons were still in pursuit when she kicked her leg out and pulled her knife from her boot. Like side-mounted propellers of death, she twirled the blades next to her and sliced deeply into the doppelgängers. Two curtains of blood coated her from head to foot, turning her landing into a sloppy sliding mess.

She needed to move to a position that would let her line up the devil with Bart, but the direction of her attack put her farther from her destination. Until the two were in position, there was no point in decapitating the demons. With her knife in one hand and the sword in the other, she rushed the disoriented pair and disgorged their guts. She didn't stop running until she caught sight of the hole in the wall alongside her.

"Done already? I was just starting to have some fun," she taunted.

The two struggled back to their feet with their entrails dangling over their belts.

"Looks like you're at a disadvantage, my dear brother," she called out. She needed to keep the little demonic fuckers alive. So long as Devlin had to deal with his troops, the devil wouldn't be able to completely focus on her. She sidestepped along the pillars until she was hidden from the demons. With a quick check of the hole in the wall, she saw Bart nod his readiness.

The two lurched out into the open, trailing blood and guts. She honestly felt bad for them. Their mission had been to guard Devlin's doppelgänger and provide security for Marjory's little event. Now that their tasks were completed, instead of being given the lives of their reals that they had undoubtedly been promised, they were being sacrificed like chickens at a voodoo ceremony.

She stepped in front of them. At the very least, they had a right to face their executioner. She pointed her blades at them. "Better luck next time, boys."

Before she could rush the two, however, Devlin swooped in from behind, grabbed their knives from their hands, and lopped off their heads. Body parts, blood, and gore lay at his feet. "Hello, sister."

With her enhanced connection to Bart, she could feel him demanding she step aside to give him a clear shot at the devil. That was the plan. "So what are you supposed to be—Malveaux devil 2.0? I think most people would consider one attempt more than sufficient." She swung her blades, hoping for a fight.

"And what about you?" He pointed his knives at the gore on the floor. "To our doppelgänger brethren, you're the true evil. Who gave you authority over the damned?" His words cut to her soul.

"I'm no angel. That's true."

"Good and evil are merely matters of perspective in an unnecessary dichotomy. We are the only two living gods on Earth with the power of overcoming death. Why should we deny life everlasting to others? By uniting human and doppelgänger, we could defeat the loas of the dead. Join me, sister."

She'd already outlived Joe. That was a pain she doubted would ever let go of her soul. Losing Bart—either to old age or battle—would be inevitable. And how was she supposed to deal with her own appearance? Maintaining her midtwenties while those around her grew old would only draw attention to her immortality, but following Jennifer's lead by accepting the wrinkles, gray hair, and infirmity of age seemed foolhardy. Then there were the loas to consider.

"Sounds like something my father would have said." Her rejoinder sounded weak even to her own ears.

"Your father sought to rule in the depravity of hell. I prefer the luxuries of life."

"But like my father, do you intend on having those you

save bow down to you?" She edged toward the next pillar while keeping her sword aimed at Devlin.

"Immortality must come at the price of submission. Otherwise, everyone would consider themselves gods."

She began to hear the familiar family foolishness in Devlin's desire to control all he surveyed. "And to those unwilling to pay your price—what would you do with those who remain mortal?"

He smiled with the same lecherous grin she'd seen from her father. "Gods deserve to have their servants."

"Slaves, you mean." As she took another half step toward the pillar, a gunshot rang out. The bullet passed so close to her neck that she felt its breeze touch the tips of her hair.

Devlin grasped his chest and laughed. "That hurt, but how could you think a bullet would harm me?" Blood spewed between his fingers.

"Just slowing you down a little." She swung her sword at his throat.

Devlin ducked and lifted one of his knives to deflect her blow. Though the defense was effective, it showed a lack of finesse. As he stood back to face her, she got a good look at the bullet wound. The hole revealed crushed ribs. Somewhere under the gore, a small paranormal pellet was working its way into his heart.

"Too bad no one taught you how to fight," Sere said. "Relying on your immortality is going to prove your undoing." Her knife, in one hand, clashed against his as her sword sliced open his abdomen. As with his use of the demons, he only knew how to operate one weapon at a time.

Like a ballerina of death, Sere pirouetted and flew through the air, slashing with her sword and knife as if they were extensions of her arms. With each of her landings, another piece of severed devil splattered against the concrete pillars and walls. But with every deadly cut, Devlin merely laughed.

Down to only one functional arm, Devlin parried another vicious sword blow to his ribs. "You can't kill me."

"I can sure as hell try," Sere grunted as she followed up her latest missed strike with a knife jab to his guts.

"So is this what we'll be to each other? Two immortals locked in never-ending combat?" He swung away from her next attack like a beat-up punching bag spewing blood instead of sand.

"If that's how it has to be, but I wouldn't rely too much on your invincibility." She dropped her knife and gripped the sword with both hands. Using all of her hundred-and-nine-pound frame, she slashed the blade cleanly through the muscles and vertebrae of his neck. Devlin's head hit the concrete floor like a dropped bowling ball. She didn't wait to see if the severed head would continue taunting her. Aiming the sword down, she drove the tip between his eyes so hard the blade sank six inches into the concrete floor.

THE CLACKING of Marjory Laroque's cane filled the basement. "You made quite the mess, little girl."

Sere picked up her knife—the Ranger blade she'd earned from Joe so long ago. If there was ever a living person she wanted to kill, it was Marjory Laroque—the person ultimately responsible for Joe's death. "You've lost, old woman."

The leader of the Laroque dynasty emerged from behind a column and stepped carefully around the pools of blood. Not a drop had splattered onto her tailored suit. "You mean this?" She aimed her cane at the carnage. "This is just a minor setback. Any man who can't pull himself together after fighting a mere waif of a girl isn't worthy to be called my heir. Devlin will either rise to the occasion, or I'll create another beneficiary of my power. Lord knows I've got plenty of relatives to choose from."

From behind her, Sere could sense Bart itching to let loose another round from his handgun. Killing the old woman would be the easiest solution, but Marjory wielded too much power to let Bart risk his life for a momentary gain. In the Laroque family, there was always someone waiting in the wings to take charge.

Sere tried not to smile. It would be a waste of time for Marjory to put her monster back together—time that would give Polly and the professor an opportunity to figure out a more permanent solution to hell's rift. And even if the Laroque matriarch were able to cobble Devlin back into a devil, he'd still be at the mercy of the pellet lodged in his heart.

Sere pointed her knife at the old woman as if she were a threat. "If he comes back, I'll just slice him up again—or maybe I should end your attempts right now."

The woman's laugh had the same devilish taunt as Devlin's. "You won't kill a human being."

Sere had used the threat of killing a real on plenty of doppelgängers as if the actual person was some unseen light casting the shadowy creature. Flipping off the switch would return the silhouette demon to the oblivion of night. Dark as Marjory's soul was, she was still a living being. Crossing the line from demon hunter to human assassin would make Sere no better than the demons she railed against. She lowered her blade. "I'm not going to kill you, but don't make the mistake of thinking I'm letting you live out of honor or mercy."

Marjory cocked her head as if trying to read Sere's thoughts. "Out of fear, then?"

The woman's words were like a dagger of ice plunged into Sere's heart. She hadn't considered that the bridge the woman had created wasn't simply for raising the dead. In place of Sere's father as hell's devil, killing Marjory might establish her as the new ruler of the underworld. *Damn it! I hope the professor learned something useful by allowing Devlin's creation.*

"Your power in life wouldn't do you much good in hell."

The woman shrugged. "And you're some kind of expert on what our ancestor achieved? Maybe you did have a front row seat, but you were a child. I've got his playbooks. We're in a multidimensional chess match, and you keep seeing my moves in terms of what checkers piece you could take off the board next. You're outmaneuvered, little girl."

Sere aimed her knife at the carnage on the floor. "And yet you're the one standing in the blood and guts of your latest *success*."

"Not all experiments yield desired results. I'm pretty

sure resurrecting you from the dead hasn't lived up to your father's hopes. If Devlin can't get it together, you will have done me a favor by ending his existence. You're not *winning* —you're simply cleaning up my failures."

Despite any advantages Marjory might have gained, however, Sere wasn't alone in her efforts. Like Baron Malveaux, Marjory thought she could play the game on her own. "A stalemate, then. I won't kill you, and you have nothing you can use against me."

"For the time being."

The black dress, blouse, and nylons that Kendell had insisted on buying for Sere made her feel like she was living some scene out of Jennifer Cranston's life. "It was a nice service." Walking next to Bart, they followed far enough back from Joe's second line down Dauphine Street that few would consider them part of the procession. For just a moment, Sere felt as if they were just like any other couple.

Bart had the sleeves of his black dress shirt rolled up halfway to his elbows. His black tie looked like a pull tab designed for quick clothing removal. "I'm sorry you had to hide among the tomes," he said. "I would have joined you."

She leaned into his solid body and reached over to flick the end of his tie, wishing she could entice him back to her apartment instead of heading to the wake. "I know you would have, but you do kind of stand out. With so many members of the Laroque family in attendance, I didn't want the solemn affair to turn into a city-of-the-dead street brawl. You did look very dashing next to Kendell and Myles."

"At least Marjory Laroque didn't show up."

Sere wasn't in any hurry to go up against the old woman again. "She's probably busy putting her humpty-dumpty of a devil back together again."

"Without the benefit of all the king's horses and all the king's men. Speaking of which, I'm glad the force sent Joe off in style. Only true comrades in arms understand what it is to lose one of their own. That's a bond Marjory Laroque will never experience."

Sere understood both perspectives all too well. She'd tried going it alone in the hope that she could keep those who cared about her from harm. People had died anyway. At least letting people in gave her a sense of belonging, even if the results weren't much different. Many of the people at the funeral, however, didn't even realize the dangers faced by those keeping the peace.

"I doubt half of the people in attendance even knew who Joe was, let alone what he did for this city." Two blocks ahead of them, the band at the front of the second line made a right toward Bourbon Street, leading the revelers to the bars like pied pipers enticing rats to their drowning.

"At least at the Scratchy Dog Joe will be remembered by friends." Bart's arm around her waist seemed so natural she wondered why she'd delayed their romance for so long.

"Then what?" She'd carefully avoided asking about when he intended to leave again, but the longer she waited to find out, the sooner the departure seemed.

He looked up into the sky as if the clouds were spelling out an answer. "I don't know. I thought I might see if Myles could use some help behind the bar. I wouldn't want to miss the next raising of the devil."

She couldn't restrain herself. She hopped and bounded in front of Bart then jumped into his arms and wrapped her legs around his waist. "You mean it? You're not rushing off?"

He held her by the ass like he was ready to make love to her right there in the street. "Not until you're ready to return to the swamp with me. Until then, I thought you could use a sparring partner to help train the Dooly Doodlebug twins."

Sere dropped her head to his chest. "I know I've never said it before, but your help means the world to me. And I don't even feel weak by admitting it."

He leaned his head to the side and kissed her neck, sending electric sparks down her spine. "You're a badass demon-hunting superheroine, but even immortals could use a hand once in a while. I'm just honored to be among those you turn to."

"You're a fucking hell of a lot more than that." She jumped down off him and pulled him into a dark doorway. "Now, kiss me like we are making love."

SERE NURSED her Jameson's whiskey while watching Polly Urethane and the Strippers perform one of their rare reunion gigs on stage at the Scratchy Dog in honor of Joe's passing. Kendell, as lead guitarist Olympia Stain, wore a skimpy black dress with torn fishnet stockings. The dress was so short that the bottom of her black electric guitar hung lower than the hem. Even in their forties, the women could belt out a number while looking sexy as hell. Myles hadn't taken his eyes off Kendell once all night except to mix drinks.

Sitting at the back of the room, Fisher bobbed to the music, dancing in a seated position. Instead of chastising him for mentally reliving his days hanging out next to the stage, crushing on each member of the band, Ann snuggled close to him on the green velvet couch and held his hand in her lap. They reminded Sere of teenage lovers who'd escaped the supervision of their families.

Sere turned to Myles. "I can't remember Joe ever cutting loose, but I think he would have really enjoyed this."

He freshened up her drink and leaned across the bar. "I checked in on the loas. They gave him a second line straight through the gates of Guinee. His soul is at rest in the *deep waters*."

Tears came so fast to her eyes that she feared she might not be able to contain the gusher of emotion. "Thanks" was all she could manage.

Bart leaned in conspiratorially. "What was all that stuff Devlin was saying about overcoming the loas?"

Though she was grateful they'd seen to Joe's passing, dealing with the lords of the afterlife always sent a chill down her spine. Having something to focus on other than Joe, however, helped her control her grief. "It was an idea my father had. He thought he could save people from death. Of course, that would only apply to the recently deceased, but then, he thought he had an eternity to work his plan. Those who didn't submit would die and live again—with each reincarnation giving him a new opportunity to win them over. Eventually, every soul would be drained from the *deep waters,* leaving the loas with nothing to do."

Myles pointed his bottle of Abita at her. "That's why the loas are so afraid of you."

She'd never considered that they might be as spooked by her as she was by them. "What do you mean? I thought they just wanted my soul for their collection."

"If people accept the idea that death isn't a given, eventually, they'll figure out a way to defeat it—with or without the help of a devil. Then Guinee will become a ghost town without any ghosts. Immortality is the great equalizer between people and the gods. And if people have an example like you, the concept of defeating death will become more than theoretical. *That's* what scares the loas of the dead shitless."

Sere really couldn't have cared less about what the loas felt. She put her drink on the bar and took Bart's hand. "I'm done saving the world for today. Dance with me."

He smiled and set his Jack and Coke next to her drink. "Whatever my sexy demon huntress wants."

Out on the dance floor, Bart wrapped his arms around her waist and twirled her in the air. With her arms spread wide, Sere felt as if the burdens of her life were flying out of her fingers to be shared by those she loved. Only by letting go of the responsibilities she felt were her birthright could she find room to let those she loved into her soul. As the song grew in intensity, Bart moved his hands to her hips and lifted her until she felt like she was flying free from the devil and the hell that had unfairly claimed her.

When the music ended, Bart swung her around as if she were weightless and lowered her against his body. She leaned her head on his shoulder and put her hands on top of his around her waist. "Take me home."

BOOK LIST

Technopia Series:
(writing as Greg Chase)
Creation
Evolution
Damnation
Salvation

The Malveaux Curse Mysteries :
(writing as G.A. Chase)
Dog Days of Voodoo
You, Me, and the Voodoo Queen
Oops! I Voodooed Again
Voodoo You Love
Voodoo You Think You Are
Look What You Made Me Voodoo
Love Me Like Voodoo

The Devil's Daughter:
(writing as G.A. Chase)
Hell in a Head Gasket
Hell Bent for Demons
Hell's Highway

<u>Other Stories</u>
Through the Lens

ABOUT THE AUTHOR

G.A. Chase is the pen name for Greg Chase. He is a science fiction and paranormal author living in New Orleans with his wife, fellow author Deanna Chase, and their two shih tzu dogs. On any given day you can find him behind his computer, people watching in the Quarter, or out in his studio creating stories in glass. His glass work can be found at www.chase-designs.com.

www.gregchaseauthor.com